TRAIL BLAZER

A LESBIAN ROMANCE NOVEL

NICOLETTE DANE

TRAIL BLAZER

As her birthday approaches, Gretchen Slate is looking to do something big. Gretchen is an avid hiker, a lover of the outdoors, and sets her sights on Maine's 100 Mile Wilderness, an arduous and remote hike far away from civilization. And she can think of no better company than her best friend Naomi Benson.

This hike is known to change people, and Naomi is in need of a change. She's never left home, never applied herself, and never admitted her true feelings for Gretchen. In fact, Naomi has spent her life running away from her feelings. While Gretchen is eager to get into the woods and climb mountains, Naomi has her own inner mountains to climb.

Out in the wild, it's easy to open up and be your real self. Can these two friends bring the love they feel in the wilderness with them when they return home?

CONTENTS

ABOUT THE AUTHOR

Nicolette Dane landed in Chicago after studying writing in New York City. Flitting in and out of various jobs without finding her place, Nico decided to choose herself and commit to writing full-time. Her stories are contemporary scenarios of blossoming lesbian romance and voyeuristic tales meant to give you a peep show into the lives of sensual and complicated women. If you're a fan of uplifting and steamy lesbian passion, you've found your new favorite author.

www.nicolettedane.com

SIGN UP FOR NICO'S MAILING LIST!

If you'd like to be notified of all new releases from Nicolette Dane and receive FREE books, head over to Nico's website and sign up for her mailing list right now!

www.nicolettedane.com

ONE

Only a few sunbeams cut through the canopy of trees. There were cottonwoods and birch and sugar maples and jack pines, the latter of which had littered the trail with dried needles over the years to make a nice buoyant path underfoot. It was a warm summer day, though deep in this forest it was cool. There were birds singing, and a wood pecker could be heard in the distance pecking relentlessly into one of the tall trees. Gretchen Slate paused in her stride, taking it all in. She looked around with a pleased smile on her face. She was by herself on this trail and it felt like hers and hers alone

Gretchen was dressed in short khaki shorts, a thin white t-shirt, and low-profile hiking shoes on her feet. She wore a close-fitted sling backpack in bright green, its asymmetrical harness wrapping around her body. A baseball cap tamed her blonde hair. Peering out from the pocket of her shorts was the clip of a knife. Partnered with the confident expression on her face, Gretchen looked like she belonged. It was obvious she knew this trail system, and that she had thoroughly explored it. And if there had been any eyes on her, they could tell that hiking was one of her passions. She loved it. This outdoor life was one of the reasons she had moved so far up north.

It had only been a year since Gretchen moved from Lansing, where she had grown up, to Traverse City. But she was ready for a change. In her twenty-nine years of life, she had lived in Lansing—and for a short time, East Lansing, when she went to college. Although she had taken road trips and explored, heading down to the Smokies or out west to the Rockies, Gretchen had never pulled up her stakes and made a move to a place that called to her adventurous spirit. But she had promised herself, about to enter her thirties, that she was going to start taking more chances and see where it lead her. Traverse City, one of the most beautiful places in Michigan's Lower Peninsula, was where her spirit took her.

There was a lot to explore in the area, most notably Sleeping Bear Dunes, the gorgeous national lakeshore on the north west side of the state. Throughout Grand Traverse County and Benzie County and Leelanau County, and further out still, there was plenty of hiking and outdoor exploration to be had. There was camping, fishing, hunting if you were into it. Even in the winter, when the ground would often be covered with multiple feet of snow, there was so much to go out and do if you were game for it. And Gretchen was game. She reveled in this outdoor living. It revitalized her. It made her feel at peace.

Before moving to Traverse City, Gretchen had rented a house in Lansing with a friend and worked as a teller for the local college credit union. It wasn't a bad life, but it was a bit boring to her. Working her full-time job, living in a place that felt less inspiring with every passing year, cycling through girlfriends but none of them panning out, Gretchen knew she needed a change of latitude. The last straw was when she had a conversation with a work friend of hers, a loan officer for the credit union.

"I don't know, Dale," said Gretchen, wearing slacks, heels, and a blue button down, a far cry from her preferred mode of dress. She looked down into the brochure that her friend had handed her.

"You should really think about it, Gretch," said Dale. "You've got great credit, no debt, and a stable job here at the credit union. You could buy something in Lansing cheap—a fixer-upper—put some work into it, and really boost your equity. You're just throwing money away renting."

"I just never really saw myself *owning* a house in Lansing," she countered.

"But you've lived here your whole life," said Dale. "Right? You don't really have any plans to leave. You should really think about it," he reiterated. "I'm telling you. You'll regret it if you don't."

"I don't feel like I can afford it," Gretchen continued. "I'm just one woman. A mortgage is a big commitment for a single salary."

"I'm telling you that you *can* afford it," said Dale. "You know I've been trying to push this on you for a while. You'll get approved easily. It's a no brainer, really."

"Let me think about it some more," Gretchen replied with a half-smile, holding the brochure up. "I'll get back to you soon."

"All right," said Dale. "My office is always open."

But Gretchen never went to Dale's office to speak to him about a mortgage. Instead, that night after Dale's latest attempt to sell her a big load of debt, Gretchen sat down at her kitchen table with a notepad and took stock of her life. She made a pro and con list of her life in Lansing. By many measures, she had it good. A stable job, friends, her family lived close by. But she wanted something different. She wasn't sure what different was, but she knew she had to try to find her place while she was still young and free.

Before she knew it, her stuff was packed up in boxes and bags and she rented a one-bedroom apartment up in Traverse City with her savings. It was a large apartment complex called Timberline, surrounded by a winding trail system. Gretchen had picked this spot precisely because of the trails all around it. It was only a few miles of paths, but it was nice to have it available in her backyard. She had quit her job, but instead of getting another teller job at another credit union up north, Gretchen decided to take on a couple part-time jobs to free her up for more adventures during the weekdays.

As Gretchen made her way out of the forest, the buildings of the Timberline complex coming into view, she looked down at her watch. There was still plenty of time to get home and shower before she had to get to work at noon. And lucky enough for her, work was just across the street from the complex. Her new work life was a breath of fresh air compared to where she had come from. Things were easy and laid-back, friendly and jovial. She could dress how she wanted and have conversations with the customers. The money wasn't as good, obviously, but it was a job that matched the lifestyle she was trying to build for herself.

After peeling out of her sweaty hiking clothes and cleaning up, Gretchen traipsed across a small plot of land in front of Timberline and approached a road. She wore beige linen pants, sandals, a black sleeveless top, and had her blonde hair in a single braid. Looking both ways, she walked across the road and towards a yellow building that looked like an A-frame barn. This was Dune City Brewing, and Gretchen poured beers here. It was only a tasting room, and because of that it was a far easier job than it might be if she were a server or bartender at a full restaurant. During most of the year, Dune City was a place for local regulars. But during the summer, it catered to its fair share of tourists as well.

It was still early, and the parking lot was empty. Dune City was only just about to open, and it would probably be another hour before anybody showed up. It was a Tuesday, after all. But you never knew in the summer when you might get blasted with customers. A brew bus might pull up and unload on them. Or a bunch of the local retirees might get thirsty and all come up at once.

Gretchen walked through the front doors with a smile on her face. It was a new thing for her to really enjoy coming into work. There wasn't much stress working at Dune City. As long as she was friendly with everybody, as long as she had a good grasp on the beer selection, she could work as much or as little as she liked. And thanks to working at Dune City, Gretchen had met her now best friend up in Traverse City, Naomi Benson.

Naomi was pretty and outgoing, and was twenty-nine just like Gretchen. She had dark hair, almost black in certain lights, pale skin, and green eyes with light freckling underneath them. Traverse City had been her home for her entire life, and she had been the perfect person for Gretchen to befriend after moving up without knowing anyone. In the short time that Gretchen had lived here, the two had become best friends. And it made Gretchen happy to walk into Dune City and see Naomi behind the counter.

"There she is!" called Naomi, holding up a white bar towel.

"I have arrived," replied Gretchen, offering a mock-curtsy, her linen pants billowing out as she did.

"Are you ready to spend ten hours together?" asked Naomi as Gretchen approached and sauntered around to join her behind the bar.

"Always," said Gretchen, stepping forward and hugging her friend. The two embraced tightly and happily.

"You smell nice," said Naomi with a smile, stepping back as their hug ended.

"I just showered," said Gretchen. "You should have smelled me after my hike." Naomi laughed.

"Or after our shift," she joked.

"Right," agreed Gretchen. "This is probably the best I'll smell all day." Naomi laughed once again.

The two women smiled together. But Gretchen's smile had a deeper adoration behind it. Ever since meeting Naomi a year prior, Gretchen had had a crush on her friend. But it was not to be. Despite never having a boyfriend during Gretchen's time knowing her, Naomi was straight. At least that's what she said. Sometimes she said things and acted otherwise—much like her compliment during their hug—but when it came to romance, Naomi seemed strangely closed off. So Gretchen simply resigned to having a great best friend in Naomi. And that would have to be good enough.

"Oh!" said Naomi. "We've got a new cherry rhubarb ale you should try. Just tapped. It's awesome."

"Pour me a taster," Gretchen said, still smiling.

Naomi nodded quickly and hopped to it, looking cute in her skinny jeans and tank top, and Gretchen just watched her with a song singing in her heart.

AFTER A LONG DAY at the brewery, Naomi drove up the driveway of her house. It wasn't actually *her* house, however. It belonged to her parents, and it was where she grew up. Approaching thirty, it made her feel pretty bad about herself that she was still living at home. But her parents insisted on it, at least until she was engaged to a "nice boy"—their words. Fortunately, there was a small cottage out back, a mother-in-law suite that was eventually meant for her grandmother, and Naomi had moved back there in her early twenties. She did pay her parents a token amount of money in rent, but it didn't blow her budget at all. Working at the brewery was enough to fund her lifestyle, and she was content with that life for the time being.

Knowing that her parents were probably upstairs asleep, Naomi casually and quietly entered the house and walked into the kitchen. There was a low light on in the hallway, a light that was always on, and following this light Naomi sauntered up to the refrigerator and yanked it open. She looked around for a moment until she spotted a rectangular glass container with a red lid on it. Pulling the container out, she then made her way over to the counter, grabbed a fork from the drawer, and opened the lid of the leftovers to find red sauce with meatballs. Naomi stuck her fork into a meatball and brought it to her mouth.

She was eager to eat quickly, and to get out of this house and back to her cottage. There was something oppressive about being in the house, and something far more liberating about being back in the cottage. The cottage was *her* space. She had her privacy. She had her freedom, no matter how truncated that freedom might be still living at home. It was back in her cottage that she could truly be herself. It wasn't something that Naomi liked to think about too often, but life in the Benson house was pretty stifled.

Just as she popped one last meatball into her mouth, Naomi heard the creaking of the staircase. She considered hurriedly putting the leftovers back into the fridge, and scurrying out of the house, but she knew she wouldn't have time to do all that before she was discovered. So instead she simply replaced the lid on the container, and went over to the sink to wash her fork. As she finished drying it and replacing it back in the silverware drawer, her mother, dressed in a matching pajama set, entered the kitchen.

"I thought I heard you come in," said her mother.

"Just stopping in for a bite," said Naomi.

"You can take that whole thing out back if you like," her mother offered.

"That's all right," Naomi said, taking the container and walking it back over to the fridge. "I'm not that hungry. Just needed a few bites."

"All right," said her mother. There was a distance between the two of them, but even though they both felt it, they both also tried to ignore it.

"I'm pretty tired, anyway," Naomi went on. "It was a ten hour shift, so I'm totally beat."

"Have you applied to any other jobs recently?" her mother asked. "Something full-time? Maybe in an office?"

"No," said Naomi. "I'm happy at the brewery."

"I have some people I could ask at church if they know of any openings," her mother continued.

"No," Naomi said again. "I appreciate it, but I'm fine right now. I'll figure it out eventually."

"If you just want to be a housewife and a mother," her

mother said with a lilt in her voice. "That's fine to admit, too. It's a noble job."

"Thanks, Mom," said Naomi. "I'm going to head out back."

"All right, dear," said her mother. "Goodnight, then. I love you."

"I love you, too," Naomi replied. She gave her mother one more smile before she turned and walked out of the house the way she had come in.

After a quick walk through the backyard, Naomi ended up at her cottage and a wave of calm washed over her upon entering. She tossed her bag down onto a small table that was positioned just off from the kitchenette and she unbuttoned her jeans. After pouring herself a glass of water, she walked into the living area, which wasn't many steps away from the kitchenette. The cottage was small, but quaint. It was the perfect size and had all the amenities that an aging woman like Naomi's grandmother would require once she could no longer take care of herself fully. Naomi knew she would have to give the spot up eventually, but for now it felt like home.

Lying on the floor in just her tank top and underwear, Naomi lifted a kettlebell weight straight up with one hand as she lightly counted the reps aloud. After doing twenty presses with her right hand, she switched sides and did the same on her left. As she did her lifts, she recalled back to the end of the night at Dune City, and she remembered Gretchen asking if she wanted to hang out.

"Come over," Gretchen had said. "Just right across the street. We'll have a beer on my porch and chill out."

"If I get home too late," lamented Naomi. "My parents will know and I'll get the third degree. You know how they are."

"Well, I've never met them," said Gretchen. "But I know how you've described them. But whatever. Come over. It's not a big deal."

"Next time," Naomi said with a weak smile. "I'll come over soon. I promise."

Naomi replayed this scene over a few times in her head as she switched hands and counted her reps. It hurt her heart that she had turned Gretchen down, but there was this strange pressure she felt in her life. It was a pressure to fit in, to be normal, and to please her parents. At almost thirty, living at home, single, working part-time at a brewery tasting room, Naomi didn't feel like she was accomplishing any of these things. And although she loved Gretchen, and felt very close to her as a friend, there was a feeling she felt around Gretchen that really made her struggle.

It was a feeling she tried to fight, but sometimes just became too overwhelming to bear. Naomi felt a pretty deep physical attraction to her pretty blonde friend. And this feeling disconcerted her to no end. It had begun the moment Naomi met Gretchen, and it intensified when Gretchen admitted to Naomi that she was gay. Naomi had known of a few gay boys when she was younger, but they weren't part of her friend group in school. Never had she known a lesbian before. She knew that was naive, that there had certainly been gay women in and out of her life even if she didn't know it, but Gretchen was the first that she had really gotten close with. And it stirred these feelings inside of her. Feelings that were hard to ignore.

After her workout was finished, Naomi headed into the bathroom to shower off for the night. She undressed completely and stepped into the shower over the small door in the sidewall. Even the bathroom had already been outfitted for its eventual inhabitant. She let the warm water course over her and stream down her pale body. As she lathered up with a hefty bar of fragrant soap, Naomi's mind once again drifted to thoughts of Gretchen. And again she regretted turning her friend down for a beer on the porch.

Soon, Naomi's thoughts played out what the night might have been like if she had taken Gretchen up on her offer. In her imagination, that beer on the porch suddenly became something more, and she imagined the two of them sitting together on the couch making out. Her heart throbbed as she dreamed this dream. As the kissing grew more passionate in her mind, Naomi began touching herself in the shower. It felt good. Really good.

She sighed and gave herself over to the feeling. Her mind raced and her fingers flicked. It didn't take very long for Naomi to bring herself to orgasm, and her legs wobbled as her middle tightened with the contractions of completion. As she composed herself, the water continuing to beat against her, Naomi steadied her breathing and tried to relax. Her cheeks were pink, her dark hair damp. Without being critical or thoughtful at all of what she had just done, she finished up her shower. When she was done, she stepped out and toweled herself off.

Looking at herself naked in the mirror, Naomi smiled gently. She felt at ease.

In order to earn enough to afford her life in the up north resort town, Gretchen also worked downtown on Front Street at a pocket knife shop called EDC in TC—Every Day Carry in Traverse City. It was a small store, with one long counter of glass display cases that held knives of all different brands and sizes. Gretchen was pretty well-versed in knives before getting the job, as pocket knives were a hobby of hers. Mostly, she loved carrying a reliable knife with her when she hiked. You never knew when a knife might come in handy.

"This is a Benchmade Griptilian 551," Gretchen said, handing the knife over to the guy standing on the other side of the counter. "Plain edge with a coated finish with 154CM stainless steel. They have a proprietary locking mechanism that's really strong, but easy to open and close one-handed."

"Huh," mused the customer. He looked at the knife and then flicked it open. After another moment of surmising the blade, he closed it.

"It's really versatile with the drop point blade," Gretchen continued. "It's a nice EDC knife, good for outdoors and hiking, and also good for tactical applications like law enforcement and military."

"What's the price?" he asked.

"That one is $100," she replied.

"What knife do you carry?" the customer said, pointing toward the clip in Gretchen's pocket.

"This," she said, pulling her knife from her pocket and opening it up. "This is the Spyderco Paramilitary 2. It's very similar to the Griptilian. They're both popular blades. CPM S30V stainless steel, compression lock, and mine has the full serrated edge because that's what I prefer for outdoor stuff." Gretchen handed the knife over to the customer.

"This is gnarly," he said, inspecting Gretchen's personal knife. He went to touch the blade.

"Careful on that one," said Gretchen. "The serrated edge can sneak up on you."

"Yeah, all right," the man replied with a slight nervous laugh. It was obvious he didn't have much experience with knives. "What does this one cost?"

"That's $130," Gretchen said. "But we don't have it in stock. We'd have to order it. The serrated edge isn't as popular as the plain edge."

"Why's that?"

"I don't know," she admitted. "Maybe because it's a little scary and harder to sharpen. Thing is, the serrated edge stays sharper a lot longer than a plain edge. I've never sharpened that one."

The man folded Gretchen's knife closed and handed it back to her. She accepted it and deftly slipped it into her pocket.

"I think I'll go with this one," he said, lifting the first knife. "I want something today, and it's cheaper."

"It's a great knife," said Gretchen. "You won't be disappointed."

After ringing the man up and packaging up the knife for him, all the while giving him more information about it and how to care for it, the door to the shop opened up and Gretchen's eyes darted over to it. When she noticed Naomi enter, a big smile moved over her face.

"Thanks a lot," said the man, offering Gretchen a wave.

"We do sharpening," Gretchen called back to the man on his way out. "If you have issues, just bring it in."

"Thank you," he said. He smiled at Gretchen, and then at Naomi on his way out. He pushed through the door and then he was gone.

"Hey," Naomi said as she sashayed up to the counter. She grinned happily and put her palms down on the glass.

"Welcome to EDC in TC," Gretchen said mockingly. "How can I help you today?"

"Hmm," Naomi said, playing along and putting a finger to her lips. "I'm looking for something that could really ruin somebody's day. Something dangerous and scary. But also dainty and girly." Gretchen laughed.

"I think I have something that would fit the bill," said Gretchen. Reaching down into the glass case, she pulled out a knife with a purple handle. Flicking it open, she handed it over to Naomi.

"Yikes," Naomi said, accepting the knife. "This looks sharp."

"Oh, it is."

"It's actually pretty nice, though," Naomi admitted. "Tell me about it."

"That's the Spyderco Delica 4," said Gretchen. "VG-10 steel, flat saber-ground, with a strong tip. And that's a 13 millimeter thumb hole in the blade for easy opening. It's a little bit smaller of a blade at 2.9 inches, but a good size for the girl on the go." Naomi laughed and then grinned.

"How in the hell do you know all this stuff?" she asked.

"I work at a knife store," Gretchen replied with a hint of sarcasm.

"This is actually a pretty cool knife," Naomi said, admiring it. "Maybe I should buy it."

"Really?" said Gretchen.

"Yeah, maybe," confirmed Naomi. "You always tell me I should carry a knife when we go on hikes. Maybe I will buy this."

"Do you care about the purple?" Gretchen asked.

"Not really," said Naomi.

"Okay," said Gretchen. She took the knife back from Naomi, folded it closed, and replaced it in the case. She then took out another knife of the same model, but this one was black. Flicking it open, it had a different blade than the first knife Naomi had seen.

"That one looks a little more like yours," Naomi said, accepting the knife from her friend.

"That's a combo edge," said Gretchen. "Half plain, half serrated. I think that's a good one for you."

"I like it," said Naomi. "It's cool. You think this would be a good one for hiking?"

"Yep," Gretchen proclaimed. "The serrated edge is good if you ever need to saw something, like rope or paracord or anything like that. It's also good for shredding zip ties and plastic. I think you'd get a lot of use out of that."

"How much?"

"It's $75," said Gretchen.

"Sold," Naomi said. She smiled happily across the counter at her friend. "I hope you get a commission for this."

"I don't," Gretchen said and laughed.

"Then I'll give you a tip," Naomi replied.

"Stop," said Gretchen, still laughing.

"A *knife* tip," continued Naomi, teasingly brandishing the knife.

"You're a nut," said Gretchen. "Put that thing away. Are you really buying it?"

"Yeah, totally," conferred Naomi. "You've told me numerous times to get a knife. So here I am, buying a knife."

"Awesome," Gretchen mused. "That's nice."

"Hey, I've got a question," said Naomi. "Knives like this are mostly a dude hobby, right? I mean, most of your customers are probably guys."

"That's right," agreed Gretchen.

"So how do they act when they come in here and see a pretty girl behind the counter?" asked Naomi. "Do they treat you like crap or what?"

"Some guys come at me with a haughty attitude,"

conferred Gretchen. "And some guys totally drool over me. But as soon as they figure out I know my shit, they get a little embarrassed and settle down really quick. I do get asked out a lot at this job."

"Yeah?" said Naomi with a laugh. "And what do you say?"

"'*I'm gay, dude*,' is what I say," Gretchen replied, also laughing. "That usually sends the turtle back into its shell."

"You're my hero," beamed Naomi happily.

"I am pretty heroic," agreed Gretchen teasingly.

"Hey, I was also thinking," Naomi said, her demeanor shifting slightly. "The other night after work. I'm sorry I didn't come over for a beer on your porch. That was really rude of me. I totally could have. I'm an adult, even if I still live at home, and I'm not ruled by my parents. I hope you weren't mad at me."

"I wasn't mad," Gretchen replied with empathy in her expression. "I understand. You still do have to play their game a little bit since you're living there. But maybe if you feel like still being at home at your age is stifling, start looking for your own place."

"It's just so expensive, though," said Naomi. "Don't you pay a grand a month for your place at Timberline?"

"Yeah," said Gretchen. "It's a lot. That's why I work two jobs. But I've also got a nice amount of savings from when I worked my full-time job in Lansing."

"I don't know how I could swing it," Naomi lamented.

"Well, there's another option," said Gretchen.

"What's that?"

"Timberline has all kinds of apartments," Gretchen said. "Maybe when my lease is up, you and I could get a two-bedroom together."

"Really?" replied Naomi with a newfound excitement. "That would be amazing."

"I think they go for like twelve or thirteen hundred," Gretchen considered. "If we split that down the middle, it wouldn't be that bad. It would save me money, too."

"I could probably do that," said Naomi. "Six hundred a month? Yeah, I think that's doable. When is your lease up?"

"I only signed a six-month term this time around," said Gretchen. "So sometime in October, I think."

"That's awesome," Naomi said. She was glowing at the thought of it. "That would be so great, Gretchen."

"Yeah, let's keep it in mind as a possibility," Gretchen said. She smiled. The idea of Naomi moving in with her, and being just down the hall, made Gretchen feel pretty excited, although she knew nothing could happen.

"Amazing," Naomi cooed, still reveling at the thought of it.

"So are you still buying this knife?" Gretchen teased with a lifted eyebrow.

"Yes!" Naomi said and laughed. "Ring me up." She tapped her palm on the glass case a few times, feigning impatience, and Gretchen just shook her head with a wide smile across her lips.

The girls had a true connection with one another.

A FEW NIGHTS LATER, after another joint shift at Dune City, Gretchen and Naomi took Naomi's car across the street to Gretchen's apartment at the Timberline complex. There was a spot just out front, and as they walked up the outdoor stairs together they filled the air with chatter and laughter. Even though it was coming up on eleven at night, there was still a hint of pink light on the horizon just over the trees beyond the complex. The sun set late in Traverse City in summer.

Gretchen's apartment was small, but modern. The kitchen and living area were in the same room, with a tall bar-style counter as their separator. As Gretchen stepped into the kitchen, she set a four-pack of tall-boy beers on the counter, red cans with a black plastic lid-lock. While she cracked two beers off the lid-lock and put the other two in the fridge, Naomi walked further into the living room and tossed her bag down to the couch.

"Let's go outside," Gretchen said with a smile, handing one of the beers over to Naomi. As she accepted the can and opened it, Naomi grinned happily.

The patio faced the forest in which Gretchen so often hiked, and that beautiful light above the trees offered a glimpse of the forests' canopy. The Timberline complex was big, with multiple buildings that all looked the same—grays and whites and browns with faux wood and stone accents. From their vantage, they couldn't see much of the complex. Just an empty field and the forest beyond it. Together, the two sat down at a small wrought-iron table on the patio and took gulps of their beers.

"Do you get tired of drinking Dune City beers?" Naomi asked, looking at her can.

"Not at all," said Gretchen. "I like them. Can't beat the discount we get on them, either." Naomi laughed.

"Yeah, agreed," she said. In a moment of comfortable silence, Naomi took another sip.

"My life now is so different than it used to be," Gretchen mused, happy to feel a cool breeze blowing as the evening set in. "Working at Dune City and EDC, living up here. It's awesome. I'm so glad I moved."

"I've never lived anywhere else," replied Naomi. "Traverse City is all I know, really."

"That's kind of how I was with Lansing," conferred Gretchen. "Though I did travel around the country some for hiking and camping."

"I've been down to Lansing, and to Grand Rapids," said Naomi. "And around a bit in the U.P. But that's really it. I've never left the state."

"Really?" asked Gretchen skeptically. "I didn't know that about you."

"I think I told you before," Naomi posited. "But maybe not."

"I'd probably remember if you told me that," said Gretchen. "So, *really*? You've never left Michigan?"

"Never," said Naomi with a sip and a smile.

"That's wild," Gretchen admitted.

"It's a tight community up here," said Naomi. "I think a lot of people who are from here don't see any reason to leave. It's beautiful and safe and pleasant. It's gotten a lot busier in the last decade, with an increase in tourism and people moving up."

"Like me," Gretchen butted in with a grin.

"Like you," Naomi said and laughed. "But I'm glad you're here."

"Me too."

"But yeah, I mean, I just never quite felt the need to go anywhere," said Naomi. "It's comfortable here."

"We should go somewhere, though," said Gretchen. "Just to experience something different. I think you'd enjoy it."

"I probably would," Naomi agreed. She smiled simply.

"You know," Gretchen said, setting her beer can down on the table and leaning in. "I've been thinking about taking a trip for my birthday next month. There's a big hike I want to do."

"Yeah?" replied Naomi. "What's that?"

"You've heard of the Appalachian Trail, right?"

"Yes," said Naomi.

"Well, *not* that," Gretchen said and laughed. "That takes months. But at the northern end of the trail, there's a hike called the 100 Mile Wilderness. It's a very remote hike through central Maine. It takes six, seven, maybe eight days depending on how fast you go. There's no civilization. You have to bring all your food with you, though I've read you can hire somebody to bring you a food resupply around the midpoint. But otherwise, you're just hiking and camping in a remote wilderness for a week. It's supposed to be really beautiful."

"Hmm," intoned Naomi. "That's something you want to do?"

"Definitely," said Gretchen. "I mean, one day I hope to do the entire Appalachian Trail, from Georgia to Maine, but I'm willing to settle for the 100 Mile Wilderness right now. Besides, it would be a nice time to do it. Since most hikers do the Appalachian northbound, they generally don't hit Maine until later on in the season."

"That sounds cool," Naomi replied. "If it's a birthday present you want to give to yourself, you should do it."

"No," countered Gretchen. "*We* should do it."

"*We?*"

"Yeah," Gretchen said with a satisfied smile. "You should come with me."

"A week-long hike?" asked Naomi. "Gretchen, I am not as experienced as you with this stuff. I don't know if I could handle it."

"You absolutely could," said Gretchen. "You're in shape. You're a runner. You work out, right?"

"Yeah, but just casually," Naomi dithered. "I'm not like a marathoner or anything."

"My point is that you could do it with your level of fitness," Gretchen said. "It will be hard, but you'll make it. It's more mental than anything."

"I don't know if I have the mental fortitude either," Naomi joked.

"Come on," Gretchen said with a smile.

"That's crazy," pondered Naomi as she thought about it more. "A week-long hike in a remote wilderness in

Maine. That's so crazy to me. How would we even get there?"

"I looked it up," said Gretchen. "We could fly Traverse City to Chicago, Chicago to Bangor, Maine. Then we'd have to catch some kind of van to Monson, Maine where the trail starts."

"I just don't know," Naomi wavered once again. "It sounds cool, I'm just not so confident in myself that I could do it. Do you think we could even get the time off work together?"

"I'm not worried about work at all," said Gretchen. "Jim is cool, he'll easily be able to get our shifts covered. And my boss Nick at the knife shop will be fine with it, too. That's the best part of having these part-time lifestyle jobs. Easy to take off from if you need to."

"I'd really have to think about it," said Naomi. She was obviously nervous about committing to such an adventure. "It's way outside my comfort zone, you know? I don't even have all the gear I would need, plus I'm sure the plane ticket will be expensive."

"I've got a ton of gear," said Gretchen. "You won't really need to buy much at all if you don't want to. I've got technical clothes that would fit you, I've got a spare backpack. We might have to get a few things, but it won't cost all that much. The flight will be a bit of money, plus we'll probably end up spending the first and last nights in a hostel in Monson. But come on. It'll be an amazing experience. You won't regret it."

"You're really giving me the hard sell here, aren't you?"

"Yes," Gretchen admitted and smiled. "That's because I want you to come."

"Ugh," Naomi groaned, tossing her head back and looking upward as she considered it all. It did sound like a difficult hike, but it would be something that would certainly pull her out of the life she was used to. And to spend that amount of time alone with Gretchen, that would be a nice bonus as well. Naomi was eager to spend as much time with her friend as she could.

"Pretty please?" begged Gretchen. "It'll be your birthday present to me."

"Okay," Naomi finally accepted. She looked across the table and smiled an agreeable smile, as though all her indecision had evaporated. "I'll do it."

"You will?" beamed Gretchen. "That's awesome, Naomi! Yes!"

"My birthday present to you," Naomi continued. She held up her beer can and hoisted it toward Gretchen.

"Cheers!" Gretchen called, knocking her can against Naomi's. They each took a gulp of beer.

"Cheers," Naomi said after swallowing, wiping at her mouth with the back of her hand.

"I'm going to start researching more tomorrow," Gretchen said enthusiastically. "I'll get everything planned out. You don't have to do a thing. We'll do a couple all-day hikes through Sleeping Bear as practice with our packs fully loaded. This is going to be great, Naomi. I am so excited!"

Naomi gave her friend a reassuring smile, and she took another drink for courage. Though her own anxiety about agreeing to this adventure was converging with Gretchen's excitement. This trip could actually turn out to be something very special.

GRETCHEN BEGAN PLANNING the trip right away. Her birthday wasn't too far off—the middle of August—and the idea was that they would walk their last day of the 100 Mile Wilderness hike on her birthday. She wanted to remove any stress of planning from Naomi, and instead help her focus on the actual physicality of the adventure on which they were about to embark. It would be a test of both outward and inward strength. It would push both to their limits. The exciting part was discovering what might await them at those limits.

To prepare, Gretchen and Naomi resolved to get outdoors and fit in a handful of hikes before tackling the 100 Mile Wilderness. Before any joint shifts at Dune City, Naomi would come by Gretchen's apartment early and the two of them would head out on the trail system surrounding the complex. It wasn't much of a distance, just a handful of miles, but it was an opportunity for them to test out the gear they might take to Maine with them. And it was an opportunity for them to talk further about the impending trek, and figure out how they might best navigate it together.

It was a weekday morning, a day both of them had off from work, and they drove out to the Lake Ann Loop. It was only about a three mile hike, but it was a beautiful location among a thick forest, rivers, and lakes. The morning was warm, and the girls dressed accordingly in shorts and tanks. They both wore backpacks, though they weren't as loaded down as they would be for the main event. Although they weren't the only people traversing the trail, it wasn't as busy as it might ordinarily be on a weekend in the middle of summer.

"How are you liking those new shoes?" Gretchen asked. Naomi looked down at her feet as she walked.

"They're great," she replied. "Much better than my sneakers. When I hit my toe on a rock or a tree root, it doesn't hurt!"

"Right," said Gretchen with a short laugh. "It's good to have shoes actually meant for hiking."

"They seem like they'll hold up well," said Naomi. With her hands gripping to the straps of her backpack, her eyes returned to the trail and she continued on.

"We should also get you some sandals," said Gretchen. "There will be some rivers we have to ford on the hike."

"What does that mean?" asked Naomi. "Ford?"

"Just... hike through," Gretchen clarified. "We'll have to walk through the water. You probably won't want to get your shoes and socks wet. So if we get some sandals, it'll make it easier. Plus, I'm sure there will be times when your feet are really hurting and you'll just want something lighter."

"You think it's going to be bad?"

"It could get bad," said Gretchen. "Blisters. Cramps. I

mean, we're hiking a hundred miles in a week. Start preparing mentally for it now."

"Have you ever done anything this long?" Naomi questioned.

"Never," admitted Gretchen. "But that's why it's so enticing to me. It's like a spiritual journey."

"I hope it is," said Naomi. She smiled softly.

"Another thing I wanted to mention," Gretchen went on, a curious smile moving across her lips. "Is trail names."

"What?"

"Well, a lot of hikers go by trail names when on the trail," said Gretchen. "It's a way to set you apart from others, and to show your personality. Some people just pick something to go by, others let the name come to them on the trail. It's up to you if you want to come up with something or let it happen naturally."

"Do you have a trail name?" asked Naomi.

"I've never really done a long enough hike for it to be a thing," said Gretchen. "But I did have a nickname in college that a lot of old friends know me as. So I'll probably go by that."

"And what is that?"

"It's kind of embarrassing," Gretchen replied, laughing at the thought of it. "Piggy."

"*Piggy*?" said Naomi skeptically.

"Yeah, Piggy," said Gretchen. "Like Miss Piggy. Or just Piggy. Or whatever. I got the name when I lived in the dorms because I would absolutely scarf down my food at the cafeteria. I've always been pretty athletic, so when it comes time to eat, I'm ravenous. I don't eat slow. And I'm blonde, like Miss Piggy." Naomi couldn't help but laugh.

"That's kind of *mean,* don't you think?" she said. "Calling you a pig?"

"I guess it carries a different connotation when the person you're calling Piggy has abs," Gretchen conferred, offering another laugh. "It wasn't a mean thing. It was just some of my teammates teasing me a bit. I like it, actually. It's accurate."

"Okay," said Naomi. "So I guess you're Piggy on the trail. What about me?"

"I don't know," said Gretchen, carefully stepping over an exposed tree root. "Do you have a nickname or something you want to be called? It could be based on something you feel defines you, or where you come from, or a trait. Anything, really."

Just then, they came to a clearing that revealed a small lake. They stepped up as close as they could to the water-front and paused in their walk, as Naomi maintained a plaintive look on her face, trying to come up with a name that might do her justice. Gretchen grinned and took a deep breath, scanning out over the calm waters in front of them.

"How about Nova?" Naomi said finally.

"Nova?" Gretchen replied. "What's the significance?"

"Sometimes I feel like I burn bright," Naomi said. "Only to soon fade away."

"That's a little sad."

"Maybe a little," admitted Naomi. "I'm still figuring out

how to stay burning bright. Maybe this hike will help me with that."

Gretchen slowly smiled, her head nodding as the idea sank in. Soon, her smile had gotten wide, her blue eyes twinkling.

"Yeah," she said with authority. "I like it. Nova."

"Piggy and Nova," said Naomi. "Sounds like a couple of expert hikers." Gretchen laughed.

"It does, doesn't it?"

After they completed the loop, the girls ended up back in the parking lot at Naomi's car. It was a small sedan, nearing a decade in age, and Naomi sat in the backseat with the door open, changing out of her hiking shoes and into some flip-flops. Gretchen stood near her, gulping water from a green-tinted wide mouth bottle. There was a oval sticker on one side of it, white with black lettering, that simply said, "TC."

Even this short hike in the summer heat had made them parched, and they worked up a nice sweat from it—especially so from carrying their backpacks. When Naomi stood up from the backseat of the car, now adorned in her flip-flops, she looked happily exhausted, her skin lightly dewy, her tank top rolled up a couple of times to expose her trim belly. Reaching out, she grabbed Gretchen's water bottle from her and took a drink.

Gretchen smiled blithely as she watched Naomi drink. She looked her up and down and felt happy. Naomi really had become her best friend. It had been a fast transition. They got along so well, they had a lot in common, and the attraction Gretchen felt for her was difficult to ignore. Although she knew nothing would ever come from it, there was always something in the back of her mind longing for more from her pretty friend. The pale face, those light freckles, that dark hair, and her big green eyes. Naomi was beautiful.

After finishing with the water, Naomi sighed at the refreshment. She caught Gretchen looking at her, and she grinned. Sticking her arm out, she handed the water bottle back to Gretchen.

"Thanks," said Naomi. "I guess I should have brought my own."

"No problem," said Gretchen. "If we don't have enough, we can stop at a gas station on the way back home to pick up some more."

"That's all right," said Naomi. "I'll manage. What are we going to do in Maine?"

"We'll bring water filtration with us," Gretchen offered. "And we'll filter water from streams."

"Is that safe?"

"Oh yeah," said Gretchen. "This is some pretty deep wilderness we're talking about. Not a lot of civilization around. The water is clear and clean. And the filters will remove any kind of sediment or bacteria or whatever that could be in it. We'll be good."

"Good to know," said Naomi. "So we won't have to worry about carrying a bunch of water with us."

"Nope," said Gretchen. "That would be pretty rough."

"It was hard enough slogging through these woods with

just that backpack on," Naomi revealed. "I don't know how I'm going to do with a bigger one. What is it, thirty or forty liters?"

"Forty-five liters," Gretchen corrected. "We're going to have a good amount of stuff. Extra clothes, first aid, minimal camping gear, food."

"Forty-five liters," Naomi repeated. She laughed. "Okay."

Gretchen grinned. Even though Naomi was often skeptical, she was agreeable just as often. She was game for whatever the plan happened to be. She had an open mind. Gretchen liked that about her. And she was certain an open mind would really help them on that arduous hike, a hike that was getting closer with every passing day.

NAOMI SAT ALONE on the wood floor of her cottage. Spread out in front of her was an unfolded map of the 100 Mile Wilderness that Gretchen had given to her. Her eyes followed along the hiking paths, mentally making notes of the various points of interest. It seemed crazy to her that they would be hiking fifteen miles or more a day, through the dense woods, over rivers, and into the mountains. There would be thousands of feet of elevation gain. Gretchen had said that, if they hiked according to plan, on one particular day they would gain almost five thousand feet in elevation.

But she also could feel the thrill and excitement of doing such a big thing overtake her. Perhaps her anxiety about it was just excitement. After all, she was fit enough. So was Gretchen, and additionally Gretchen had plenty of hiking and camping experience. She was confident and smart. There really wouldn't be anything to worry about. Maybe bears. Naomi had seen bears a few times in her life around Traverse City. Bears, far out in the wilderness, away from civilization, were a more frightening proposition, though.

It was starting to sink in that this was really happening. Gretchen had secured their plane tickets, and Naomi had already paid her back. They had gotten the time off of work. In fact, their manager Jim was enthusiastic about them going. He had always wanted to hike the Appalachian Trail himself, he knew about the 100 Mile Wilderness, and he said he was actually quite jealous that Gretchen and Naomi were doing it. All of this made Naomi's head spin. There was no going back now. This hike was happening.

Naomi rolled on her back on the floor and looked up at the ceiling, a calm smile on her face. She closed her eyes and she imagined what it would be like. In her daydream, she saw herself and Gretchen hiking along a rocky path, smiling and laughing, holding deep, meaningful, philosophical conversations. They would talk about everything. Even stuff that they had never talked about together. Really personal stuff. Secrets and inner desires. Nothing would be off the table. When you embark on such an onerous journey, you're bound to grow much closer with your company.

Further still in her day dream, Naomi imagined sharing a tent with Gretchen. It would have to be a small tent if they were to carry it on their back. Pressed up next to each other, sharing a sleeping bag, exhausted from a long day of hiking, Naomi pictured wrapping her arms around Gretchen and holding tight to her. Naturally, the two of them lightly kissed one another, but more than just a few easy pecks. The kisses felt emotionally powerful, despite their softness. And then, they would go to sleep in one another's arms, longing for a rejuvenating slumber so that they could do it all again tomorrow.

Naomi opened her eyes in a jolt, and she stared upwards at the ceiling once again. It wasn't that she wanted to *fight* those kind of thoughts. It was more that they confused her. She had gone so long defining herself as one thing, all while constantly having these thoughts deep in her mind. It had started, she remembered, in high school. There was something about one of her good friends at the time, Lily French. Lily was pretty and outgoing and blonde, a lot like Gretchen. And back then, Naomi often daydreamed about what it might be like to kiss Lily.

She kept it all bottled up. Back then, she was a lot more active in the church. She didn't have a choice, really. Her parents made her go. And on some level, she embraced it. There was a lot of camaraderie and positivity around being active with the church's youth program. They did a lot of events together, they took trips down to Grand Rapids to go to museums and concerts. But they also conferred onto Naomi that the kind of thoughts she had been having about Lily were wrong. And she took that as the truth.

Some time in her early twenties, however, Naomi fell out of the church. It just didn't seem to fit her anymore. Her parents were upset, but they allowed Naomi her freedom. Around that time, she moved out of the family house and into the cottage out back. With this move, this step toward independence, Naomi slowly dropped all the beliefs she had grown up with. She just let them go, without any fanfare. It was a natural progression, but even as she approached thirty it was still something she wrestled with.

Sitting up now, Naomi scooted over toward the small couch in her living room and sat crosslegged in front of it. On the cushion in front of her was her laptop, and she deftly opened up the screen and began to move her finger over the trackpad. At first, she brought up a search engine with the intention to suss out more information about the hike. But very quickly she found herself typing something completely different into the search bar.

"How to tell if you're bisexu--" Naomi typed. But then she stopped and she looked at the word she had half-typed. After another moment, she tapped the delete key a handful of times until that word disappeared. And in it's place, she instead wrote out, "lesbian."

The search engine returned a whole host of results, many of them seeming a bit pithy or overly simplistic. On one particular web page, a list of "ten ways to know if you're a lesbian" informed Naomi that if you find yourself wearing plaid and sneakers all the time you might be a lesbian. This made Naomi scoff. It felt so trite and superficial. Of course she wore plaid—the winters in northern Michigan were cold, and flannel shirts, often plaid, helped her keep warm. And sneakers, who didn't wear sneakers?

She then moved on to an online test to determine whether or not she was a lesbian, but she quickly gave that up. The first question, "Who do you find most attractive," immediately put a sour taste in her mouth with the available answers. Things like, "What were you saying, I was thinking about boys," and "Why would I find girls attractive, gross," along with simply "girls" as the answer most in line with what Naomi was trying to determine. This test felt like it had an agenda, so juvenile and worthless. After that, the entire prospect of using the internet to figure out her feelings seemed like a lost cause.

Perhaps these articles and questions and tests were geared for a younger audience, a crowd of girls who might need to ease into these nebulous ideas. Not a woman approaching thirty who should have a better grasp of herself. Then again, nothing about Naomi screamed adulthood apart from her age. Still living at home, still working a part-time job, still unsure of her emotions and feelings. It made Naomi feel stunted and small and alone.

Naomi closed her laptop and stood up from the floor. Looking out of the window and into her family's backyard, it was a beautiful day outside with a blue sky above and the sun shining bright. A few fluffy clouds rollicked through the vastness overhead. Below, on the ground, the grass was dark green and recently mowed. It was idyllic, really. Everything felt so natural and perfect out there. Naomi wanted to be out there, out in nature, out in the elements. She wanted to go run through the grass barefoot and feel the earth below.

But she had to go to work soon, and she knew—thankfully so—that Gretchen would be there. Naomi also knew that she had to open up to her friend. She had no other choice but to share her feelings with Gretchen, because Gretchen was the only one in her life that could help her make sense of it all. Naomi, however, was scared. She was scared of what kind of complications would emerge from admitting what she knew to be true. What would her family think? Her friends? How would her life change? And then, how would Gretchen react? Admitting to her that Naomi had feelings for her could jeopardize their relationship. And that was not something Naomi was keen to do.

It would have to wait. Naomi resolved that she would open up to Gretchen on the trail, deep in the heart of the 100 Mile Wilderness. That's where she would be safest. There would be nowhere to run and hide. All there would be was a path, putting one foot in front of the other, spilling her feelings out into the vast open emptiness of the Maine woods.

That's where Naomi could find herself.

ONCE THE DECISION was made to go on the hiking trip, the weeks started to fly by. Gretchen and Naomi were spending even more time together preparing for the trip—in addition to working together at Dune City—and they made sure they would be ready for any contingency. Fortunately, Gretchen did have most of the gear Naomi would need. They would take one small tent in case they needed it, though the 100

Mile Wilderness did have a good number of shelters for hikers and the girls would be able to string up hammocks to sleep in within the shelter walls.

The day of their flight out to Maine was closing in, and the excitement was building. It was a busy Friday evening at Dune City, and Gretchen and Naomi stood behind the counter serving patrons, alongside Jim the manager. Jim was a short, stocky guy with messy dark hair and a stubbly beard. He was in the back changing out a keg, while the girls hovered around a regular customer and chatted with him.

"We're really looking forward to it," Gretchen said to the man, who looked to be in his mid-sixties. He had a gut, white hair, and a white beard. His name was Keith.

"I can't believe the trip is almost here," mused Naomi.

"When I was younger," said Keith. "I did the John Muir Trail out in California. In the Sierra Nevadas. That's over two hundred miles. Elevation changes of over forty seven thousand feet. That was a monster hike." He sipped his beer from a mug as he ruminated.

"Wow," said Gretchen. "Yeah, I'd love to do the John Muir one day. How was it for you?"

"Well, it was a bit different when I did it," said Keith. "It was the seventies, and we didn't have all the technical gear you have today. There also wasn't the same kind of information out there for planning the hike. No internet, of course. We were kind of foolish. I survived on a lot of beef jerky." The girls laughed.

"Think you'd do it again?" Naomi asked.

"Today?" asked Keith. "No way. I'm too out of shape.

Back then, though… yeah, it was worth it. I'm glad I did it. But I never did another big hike like that again. I only did it because I was in with some extreme sports guys back then. The kind of guys who would go climbing in Yosemite before it was popular. No, I couldn't really hang with them."

"You need another?" Gretchen asked, indicating to Keith's empty glass.

"Sure," he said. "I'll have the ESB."

"You got it," replied Gretchen, taking his mug. She turned from the bar and approached the beer taps. First she washed out his mug by putting it upside down on a rinser, spraying water up into it. Then she proceeded to fill the glass with Keith's requested brew.

"Hey," said Naomi, as though she were speaking to Keith in secret. "Give it to me straight. I've never done any kind of hike like this before. Am I going to regret it?"

"Well, I don't know," Keith replied with a laugh. "In the moment, you might get a little uncomfortable. My God, the blisters. But I'm sure you all have better shoes than I did in my day. I don't think you'll regret it, though," he continued. "It really might be a life-changing experience."

"That's what I'm hoping," said Naomi with a small smile.

"When are you leaving?"

"In like a week," she said. "It's coming up quick."

"I'm guessing you're all prepared," said Keith. "You've got your gear and supplies and all that."

"We do," Naomi conferred.

"Don't stress about it," Keith said with a wave. "You'll be fine."

"ESB," Gretchen said upon returning, sliding the mug back to Keith.

"Thank you, kindly," he replied.

Jim came out from the backroom and approached a tap. He took a thin taster glass and he attempted to fill it. At first, there was an abundance of foam. He dumped that out and filled it once again, this time with actual liquid beer. Satisfied that the keg was changed over, he took the taster glass and approached another customer sitting at the bar and gave it to them free of charge.

Gretchen and Naomi wandered off from Keith, allowing him to return to a conversation he was having with another regular at the bar, and they moved over toward Jim. Dune City was busy, but everybody seemed to be well taken care of. Seeing as it was a tasting room and not an actual bar, if anybody wanted a beer, they would just have to come up and ask. No table service here.

"So are you sure you're going to be fine without us?" Naomi asked Jim.

"Oh sure," he said. "Jacob and Liz are cool to pick up your shifts. I'm just excited for you guys that you're doing this trip. I hope to see some good pictures."

"Definitely," said Gretchen. "We'll take some photos to show you."

"So what's the plan?" Jim questioned. "You're flying out next Thursday?"

"Right," Gretchen replied. "Flying out Thursday

early morning, then we should end up in Bangor by the early afternoon. Then we're taking a shuttle out to the Hiker Hostel in Monson at the start of the trail. Staying there overnight, and starting the trail on Friday."

"Nice," said Jim. "How long you think a hundred miles will take you?"

"Originally I was thinking seven days," said Gretchen. "But I read that the last half of the hike has a lot of downhill miles, so we think we can do it in six."

"Six days," said Jim. "Phew. What do *you* think?"

"I'm deferring to Gretchen," Naomi said with a laugh. "She's got the experience here. If she thinks we can do it in six, we can do it in six."

"Well, that following Wednesday is my birthday," said Gretchen. "I want to be reaching the end of the trail when I turn thirty." She grinned.

"I'm sure you can do it if you put your mind to it," admitted Jim. "I'll be thinking about you guys while you're out there. Just be careful and watch out for bears. You know to store your food up hanging in a tree, right?"

"Of course," said Gretchen with a knowing smile. "I've done plenty of camping before."

"Good," said Jim. "Well, don't worry about us back here. You girls just get in the zone and do this hike. It's a chance of a lifetime. You're going to love it."

Just then, Jim noticed that a customer had moseyed up to the bar at the opposite end. Jim raised a finger to let the man know he'd be right over.

"I'll get him," Jim said. "Be right back." He walked off to the other end of the bar.

"You all right?" Gretchen asked. "Excited?"

"Yeah," said Naomi. "Do I look all right?"

"You just have a little trepidation on your face," replied Gretchen with a laugh.

"I guess I'm a little nervous still," admitted Naomi. "Keith was just saying some stuff. And Jim talking about the bears. I know it's all going to be fine, but I just don't know what to expect."

"It's going to be great," Gretchen said with confidence, placing her hand on Naomi's shoulder. "Don't worry about a thing. We're going to have a blast."

"You don't think we'll actually end up hating one another?" Naomi quipped. Gretchen laughed once more.

"I don't think so," she said. "But hey, I guess it's possible. Maybe we'll get at each other's throats. You think?"

"No," Naomi said with a revealing smile. "I don't think we'll be at each other's throats."

"Me neither," agreed Gretchen. "It's going to bring us closer together, I'm sure. There's nothing like overcoming obstacles to bring you closer together with someone."

"What if we get hurt, you know?" Naomi posited. "Like, what if one of us falls and breaks a leg?"

"I really don't know," said Gretchen. "I've read that there are some places where you can get phone reception, so I guess we'd just have to find a pocket of reception and call 911. That's about all we could do. Or maybe another hiker on the trail could help us. But I don't think that's going to happen. We'll be careful, we'll go at a good pace, won't take too many chances. As long as we're not hiking after the sun sets, I don't think we'll stumble into any trouble."

"Right," Naomi said with a slow nod. She was smiling as she contemplated it all. It still didn't feel real. It was still only talk at this point. But the day was coming soon, just a week away, and she could feel the excitement fomenting inside of her. And she could also tell, from the look on her friend's face, that Gretchen felt the same way.

The night carried on with Gretchen and Naomi talking both with customers and with each other about their impending trip. It was all either of them could think about. Naomi's confidence in the trip and in herself built up as they spoke to more people about it. It was like vocalizing it made it all the more real. And everybody was positive about it. The fact that she was doing this, committing to it, going on this adventure with Gretchen, it made her feel like she was starting to shine bright. She was doing something meaningful and worthwhile, something to brag about when it was all said and done. And she was doing it with someone she really cared about. Someone who seemed to understand her, and would hopefully understand her even better once they finished.

Maybe Naomi would really burn bright on this trip. And hopefully she wouldn't soon fade away after it was over.

THE NIGHT BEFORE THE FLIGHT, Gretchen and Naomi hung

out at Gretchen's apartment and went through the bags they were taking on the trip. Laid out on the floor were two medium-sized backpacks, top-loading with a flap to secure them shut. Spread around the packs were all the various items the girls would need for their hike. They had lightweight rain jackets, extra underwear and sports bras, telescoping walking poles, hiking sandals made of a basic foam footbed, rubber soles, and webbed polyester straps, along with many more items for camping and trekking.

Gretchen kneeled next to a rugged duffel bag and packed it with a few ancillary items. It was to be their checked bag on the flight, as well as a bag they could leave at the Hiker Hostel with whatever they didn't want to take with them on the trip.

"We'll hide our knives in here," Gretchen said. "They should be fine to check, but we don't want some baggage handler to go searching through and swipe them."

"Does that happen?" Naomi asked, lifting a brow.

"Unfortunately," said Gretchen. "I had a friend who had some prescription medicine stolen from her checked luggage one time. It wasn't even something to get you high. It was some sort of antibiotic."

"Yikes," replied Naomi. "I hope we don't get our knives stolen."

"That would be sad," Gretchen confirmed.

"So we'll also stash our street clothes in there?" said Naomi.

"Yep," said Gretchen. "We'll have a locker at the Hiker Hostel and we can put whatever random crap we want in it.

We can also buy our food there for the hike. I had been worried about how we'd get supplies, but we can hop into a grocery store in Bangor—get some basics there—and then supplement with whatever else at the hostel. They'll also bring us the second half of our supplies midway through the hike."

"Okay," Naomi agreed. "That all sounds perfect."

"You getting nervous?" asked Gretchen with a wry grin as she stood up from the floor. "Feeling antsy?"

"A little," said Naomi. "But I'm actually feeling pretty good about it. It feels nice to be on the edge of a trip. No work for over a week, I'm staying over tonight so I don't have to head back home. It's exciting, you know?"

"You worried about the flight?"

"Naw," Naomi said, and then she paused. "I mean, yeah, sure. Only because I've never flown before. But I'm not *really* worried. I'm getting pumped for all these new experiences."

"I'm excited for you," Gretchen conferred. She stepped away from the living room and went to the refrigerator, reaching in and taking out two bottles of beer. She popped their tops with an opener. "I'm happy to be with you for all this new stuff."

"Thanks," Naomi said, accepting the beer bottle as Gretchen handed it over. "Yeah, I'm ready. I'm too old for this to be my first flight. I want to put this embarrassment behind me."

"We'll have to do something special for your birthday, too," Gretchen posited with glee. "I'll have to think about it and come up with something. Unless you already have an idea."

"My thirtieth?" responded Naomi, after taking a drink. "Yeah, but my birthday is in December. I guess we could go skiing."

"You do that every winter, though," said Gretchen. "I mean something bigger. Like, maybe we go to Mexico or something."

"Huh," mused Naomi. "Yeah, maybe."

"Well, whatever we figure out, I'm sure it'll be fun." Gretchen tossed her head back and took a pull off her beer bottle. When she was finished with her gulp, she smiled wide.

"So once we pack these bags all up, that's it," Naomi surmised, looking down at all the gear on the floor. "Next time we dig into them, we'll be on the trail."

"That's right," said Gretchen. "But I think we've got everything we need. First aid, basic shelter, we'll have food soon enough. We might catch a little bit of rain, so the rain jackets are important."

"Maps," mused Naomi, still assaying all the stuff.

"Maps," reiterated Gretchen.

"I'm just glad I'm not on my period," joked Naomi. Gretchen burst out laughing.

"God, you're so right," said Gretchen. "There is no *way* I would have scheduled this trip if I was going to be on my period."

"You ever wish you could just rip out all the plumbing down there?"

"All the time," Gretchen confided. "*I've* got no use for it," she said and laughed. "No way I'll ever get pregnant. I guess it still matters for you, though."

"Yeah," Naomi said absently.

"You ever had any scares?" Gretchen asked without pretense.

"No," said Naomi. Her response was curt and low, almost as though the topic were making her uncomfortable. Gretchen noticed immediately and backed off.

"Well, anyway," she said. "I think we've got everything, checked it twice, three times, and there's nothing left to worry about. Jim's going to drive us to the airport tomorrow morning, and we're off."

Naomi smiled, coming back around, and she stuck the neck of her beer bottle out. Gretchen smiled in kind, and she tapped the neck of her bottle against Naomi's. They both drank.

Later on, after everything had been packed up for the final time and placed expectantly near the apartment door, Gretchen and Naomi lay together in Gretchen's bed. Being this close to an undressed Gretchen sent a thrill through Naomi. And Gretchen felt the same way, but she had better learned to suppress those kind of urges for her friend. Still, there was a strange energy bouncing between the two as they lay there in the darkness, both still awake, neither sure if it was the excitement of being close to one another or the excitement for the impending trip that was keeping them up.

"Are you still up?" Naomi whispered.

"Yeah."

"Sorry," said Naomi. "I can't sleep."

"That's all right," said Gretchen. "What's on your mind?"

"Just stuff."

"Yeah," Gretchen agreed. "Me too."

"Your bed is comfortable, though," Naomi said.

"It's memory foam."

"It's nice. I should get one like this."

Gretchen felt a pang of confusion run through her. In other circumstances like this, with a cute girl in her bed, she would definitely make a move. But that obviously shouldn't happen with Naomi. What a mess *that* would be. On the evening before their big trip together, Gretchen makes some move, and gets rebuffed by her straight friend. Gretchen tried to tame her thoughts. She was stronger than this.

"You ever think that traditions and ways we're told to live," said Naomi. "Is just dead people peer pressuring us?" Gretchen laughed softly.

"Yes," she agreed. "I think that sounds about right."

"Just the weird, psychological baggage of old people," Naomi continued. "Just because they thought some way in the past, that doesn't make it necessarily correct."

"That's right."

"But when it goes on for so long," said Naomi. "When you believe it for so long, it just becomes engrained in your head. It's so hard to let it all go."

"Is there something you're trying to let go?" asked Gretchen.

"A lot of things," admitted Naomi. "A lot of my upbringing, I guess."

"I'm sorry you had such a... *traditional* upbringing."

"It's held me back a lot," said Naomi. "You know I'm named after a Biblical character, right?"

"No," said Gretchen. "I didn't know that."

"Naomi had to leave home with her husband and sons because of a famine," Naomi began. "But eventually, her husband and sons all died. She endured destitution and poverty, and she was bitter about it all. At one point, she tells people to call her Mara. I don't remember why. It must mean something in Hebrew. Maybe Mara actually means bitter."

"What does it all mean?" asked Gretchen. "Aren't those stories supposed to have a message or a moral? A parable, right?"

"I don't know," said Naomi. "The whole story seems kind of... patriarchal, in a way. Naomi ends up persuading her daughter-in-law Ruth to marry this guy, they have a kid, and then Naomi cares for him. Because they're broke, I think? I mean, she's just this woman doing what she has to do. But it all feels so submissive."

"Do you resent your name?"

"No," Naomi said plainly. "It's just a name. I think it's pretty, actually."

"It is," agreed Gretchen. "It's a nice name."

"But maybe I do sort of feel like Naomi," she said. "Bitter about certain things I had no control over. It can be hard to get over that."

"Maybe we should just call you Nova now," Gretchen softly teased, reaching over and giving Naomi's side a squeeze. This simple touch sent shivers up Naomi's spine. She reached out and took Gretchen's hand.

"Maybe I should go by Nova," said Naomi. "Not just on the trail, but in life."

"Mmm," hummed Gretchen happily, her fingers playing with Naomi's.

"I'm sorry," said Naomi, now pulling her hand back. "We should probably sleep. I didn't mean to start talking."

"That's okay," said Gretchen. Underneath the covers, she tried to once again find Naomi's hand. But it didn't want to be found.

"I'm just going to turn over," said Naomi. "I'll see you tomorrow, Gretchen."

"All right," Gretchen replied with a hint of disappointment. "I'll see you tomorrow."

"Goodnight," said Naomi.

"Goodnight."

WHEN GRETCHEN and Naomi stepped out of the airport terminal in Bangor, Maine, the sun was shining brightly and they were hit with a blast of heat and humidity. The airport was small and a little outdated, but it was nice to arrive at an airport that wasn't completely overrun with other passengers, speeding about frantically. It was generally calm at Banger International, and that made them both feel good after the insanity at O'Hare.

"I can't believe the difference," mused Naomi, looking out into the early afternoon through her sunglasses, adjusting her backpack for greater comfort. "From Cherry Capital to O'Hare to Bangor. It's all over the place."

"Yeah, O'Hare is one of the big ones," said Gretchen. "I'm glad you got to see it on your first time flying." She, too, wore a backpack and she also carried their shared duffel. Gretchen looked around outside the terminal for what might be their transportation.

"It is *hot* today," said Naomi, fanning herself off and then airing out the sleeves of her t-shirt.

"It definitely is," Gretchen aggreed absently, still looking around. She spotted a small SUV that matched the description she had of their car service. Stepping closer to it, she looked inside. Once the woman inside saw her, she grinned and waved, and then proceeded to hop out of the car and approach the girls.

"Ladies," said the woman with a pleased face and a confident tone. She was stocky, yet looked strong. "I'm Babs. Pleased to meet you."

Babs stuck out her hand and both Gretchen and Naomi shook in turn.

"Gretchen."

"Naomi."

"Hot one, isn't it?" said Babs. She removed a pink visor from her head and fanned herself off. "I've got the AC on blast in the car. Let's get your bags in there and skedaddle."

Reaching out, Babs took the duffel from Gretchen and lead them both around to the back. She opened up the rear door of the SUV, and they all loaded their bags in. Just as quickly as she'd opened the door, Babs pushed it closed with one hand.

"Get in, get in," she ushered them impatiently. "We're going to melt out here." Naomi offered a short laugh and followed their driver's command. Soon, Babs was back in the driver's seat, while the girls sat in the back.

And then they hit the road.

"Now I know you said you wanted to stop in Bangor," said Babs. It was then that the girls really started to notice Babs' accent. Her words came out more like "*staup en Bangah.*"

"Right," agreed Gretchen. "We wanted to pick up some supplies at a grocery store."

"If you gals are doing the 100 Mile Wilderness," said Babs. "There's a nice little general store in Monson that'll have everything you need. Let's get out of the city, we'll go there, then I'll take you to the Hiker Hostel."

"Yeah?" said Gretchen, looking over at Naomi. Naomi just shrugged.

"Oh yeah," said Babs, her accent really coming out again. "Monson's really coming around. Some big money is coming in to help revitalize the town. The hiking helps. And all the *otts*."

"The *otts*?" reiterated Naomi, looking to Gretchen for clarification.

"*Otts*," Gretchen said up to Babs. "What's that?"

"You know," said Babs. "*Otts. Ottists.* Painting and such. They're starting to make Monson their home."

"Oh," said Gretchen with a grin. "Arts."

"Right," replied Babs, laughing. "That's what I said." Naomi laughed as well and grinned wide, putting her hand over her mouth.

"Okay," said Gretchen. "I think we're fine with picking up supplies in Monson, if this store you know of will have everything we need."

"Oh sure," said Babs. "A lot of hikers come through, so they cater to that. You'll be fine."

"All right, then," replied Gretchen. "Cool?" she asked Naomi.

"Yeah, cool," Naomi replied.

"So where did you gals say you were from?" said Babs, looking at them through the rearview mirror as she drove.

"Traverse City, Michigan," said Gretchen. "Way up north in the Lower Peninsula."

"Oh, I bet it's beautiful up there," said Babs. "Maybe a lot like here in Maine. Though I bet Maine could give Michigan a run for its money. They don't call us Vacationland for nothing."

"We're really looking forward to the beauty here," said Naomi. "We're hoping to see a lot of it on the hike."

"Oh yeah," said Babs. "You'll bee seeing Katahdin on your hike. It's the highest mountain in Maine. But I don't think you're climbing it, are you? You're just doing the hundred miles?"

"Right," said Gretchen.

"Katahdin is the end of the Appalachian Trail," said Babs. "Maybe you'll do that all next time."

"I'd love to," replied Gretchen. "That's a big commitment."

"Yeah, my cousin and her guy did it one time," Babs revealed. "They were gone for six months. My God. When they got back to Maine, I hardly recognized them. They both lost so much weight. You gals don't have anything on you to lose. Bulk up before you go on that one. That's my advice."

"I don't think I'll be doing it," Naomi said and laughed.

"I don't blame you," said Babs. "Me neither."

"Let's see how we do on this hike before we make a decision either way," teased Gretchen, nudging Naomi softly with her elbow.

"Yeah, we'll see," Naomi replied, offering yet another laugh.

It took over an hour for them to drive from the airport out to Monson, and the ride was smooth and easy. Even on the highway, there was a lot of nature to look at. And in a way, it did feel somewhat like Northern Michigan. Babs was entertaining throughout the ride, and she either loved the sound of her own voice or was born without a vocal filter. She always had something to say and had a colorfully accented way of saying it. For some reason, Babs' accent really tickled Naomi. Although she didn't speak up as much as Gretchen did, Naomi's contribution to the conversation was usually laughter as she tried to figure out some of the words that Babs said.

The general store in downtown Monson was exactly as Babs had described it. And it was one of the only stores downtown. Conveniently enough, the general store was literally around the corner from the Hiker Hostel and the girls very well could have walked back and forth to get their supplies. But Babs insisted on waiting for them so they wouldn't have to carry their groceries and all their bags down to their accommodations. When all was said and done, Babs dropped Gretchen and Naomi off in front of the Hiker Hostel, she wished them well and waved, and then she was gone.

The hostel looked almost like an old farmhouse, with white siding and a simple screen door out front. As they entered inside, both Gretchen and Naomi got the impression that it was a relaxed sort of place. It looked like it had one time been someone's home, and it had transformed over the years into something more of an institution. It definitely gave off a hippie vibe.

As they brought their stuff inside, a woman approached them with a smile. She had dark hair pushed back with an elastic band around her forehead, small wire-framed glasses, and an olive-toned complexion. This woman exuded friendliness.

"Howdy," she said. "Welcome to the Hiker Hostel. I'm Chickie."

"Naomi," replied Naomi, smiling as she shook Chickie's hand.

"Gretchen," said Gretchen, following suit. "We talked on the phone."

"That's right!" confirmed Chickie. "You girls have a double room."

"We do," Gretchen agreed.

"Great," said Chickie. "Let's get your stuff all put away and then we can sit down and hash out your plans. You're starting tomorrow?"

"Yes," both women said at once.

"Okay, well we'll be able to help with anything you need," said Chickie. "Let's get you to your room, then I've got a cold beer or soda with your names on it."

Gretchen and Naomi both smiled. With a wave of her hand, Chickie beckoned them to follow her and they eagerly did so. Wandering throughout the Hiker Hostel, they saw a handful of other hikers just like them, sitting around and communing, talking about their hike or the hike they were about to embark upon. It was obviously a convivial group of people staying here. To Gretchen, this was exactly the kind of experience she had hoped to find herself in. And Naomi, she was pleasantly surprised and comforted by the atmosphere at the Hiker Hostel.

After ditching their bags and each being handed a beer by a large, burly man with a red beard—a man they soon discovered was Chickie's husband, and co-owner of the hostel, Bard—Gretchen and Naomi followed the couple back down into a dining room area. It all felt so exciting to be on the precipice of this new adventure. Gretchen had been enthused about it for weeks, but now she could really see the thrill in Naomi's eyes as well.

It was getting real. It wouldn't be too much longer until they were out on the trail together.

"THE BEST PLACE for us to send someone out to meet you," said Bard, sitting across the table from Gretchen and Naomi, with his wife Chickie by his side. "Would be right about here." Using a pencil, he pointed at a spot on the map that lay unfolded open on the table.

"Most likely your fourth day," Chickie said.

"How does it work?" Gretchen asked. "How will you know when to meet us?"

"It will be Theo meeting you," said Bard. "He'll be out there around noon or so and will stick around for a couple hours. Just try to land in that window. He'll know who he's delivering to. If anything changes, you can give us a call. There are spots where you'll get cell phone service."

"If you get all of your resupply stuff together in a bag," Chickie continued. "You can give it to me tonight or tomorrow morning, and that's what Theo will bring out. We'll also bring you out a complimentary beer or soda, whatever you prefer."

"Probably a beer after hiking that long," Gretchen said with a grin. "Right?"

"Yeah, a beer would be good," agreed Naomi.

"Great," said Chickie with a smile. She made a note on a piece of paper in front of her.

"At the end of your hike," said Bard. "Someone will pick you up at the Abol Bridge Campground, right here," he said, again pointing with his pencil. "It will probably be in the evening, around six or seven. If you miss that pickup, you can call us and try to schedule something for the morning. Otherwise, you'll have to wait another day to get back to the hostel."

"We can usually accommodate," said Chickie. "We try our best. But please don't be upset if you end up having to wait another day."

"It's real pretty out there at Abol Bridge," said Bard. "An extra day camping there isn't the end of the world."

"Right," Chickie agreed and smiled.

"I think we're looking at doing the entire hike in six days," said Gretchen. "Do you think that's doable for us?"

"Are you experienced?" asked Bard.

"I am," confirmed Gretchen. "I've done a lot of hiking, plenty of camping, but nothing like this before. Nothing so long in the wilderness."

"What about you?" he asked Naomi.

"I'm not as experienced as Gretchen," she said. "Just shorter hikes and some camping experience. Though I'm decently athletic."

"I think it'll be best if your resupply pack has enough food in it for four days," said Bard. "Take four days with you on your way out, pick up four days in the middle. It's better to have a little more than you need than not enough. In case you take a little longer than planned."

"The last half of the hike does have some quicker

miles," said Chickie. "But you never know how you might be feeling by then."

"Okay," said Gretchen. She looked over to Naomi and smiled. Naomi's response was a smile with a hint of worry in it.

"We have a bin of packaged food you could look through that other hikers have left," said Chickie. "And if you feel like you're missing anything, we do have some food for sale and you can always make a quick run to the general store. You have water filters, right?"

"Yes," the girls said in unison.

"You'll be fine," Chickie surmised, looking happy and kind.

"I think that's it," said Bard with finality. "Depending on how you're feeling, you could go meet some other hikers who might be heading out at the same time. Or you could do your own thing and get a shower and a good night's rest. If you need anything, one of us is always around or you could call. Any more questions?"

"I don't think so," said Gretchen. "I think I've got it." She looked to Naomi and raised a brow.

"Yeah, I'm good," said Naomi. "I'm feeling a bit nervous, but excited. Happy, you know?"

"Don't worry," Chickie said, reaching across the table and placing her hand atop Naomi's. "You'll do just fine. Just be smart and know your limits."

Naomi smiled back and she nodded in understanding.

Later on, as the sun began to set, Gretchen and Naomi

hung around in their private room, each of them going through their backpacks and making sure they had everything they needed. They both had things lying out on their beds, and they sorted through their supplies, extra clothing, various gear, everything. They were dressed down for the night, and had already packed the clothes they had worn on the flight away into their duffel bag. Treating themselves, they bought another two bottles of beer and sipped them slowly as they prepared.

"First aid kit," Gretchen mused absently, recounting her things to herself. She moved the small bag of her first aid supplies from one section of the bed to the other. "Hammock. Sleeping bag. Tent pack." Each of these things were of the very small, lightweight variety. Though every little thing added up in weight.

"I feel like we just did this last night," said Naomi.

"We did," Gretchen replied with a laugh, looking up from her work. Naomi grinned.

"I know," she said.

"We just have to make sure," Gretchen clarified. "I don't want to be out there and realize we left something important behind."

"I'm with you," Naomi agreed. "I'm just teasing you."

"You're cool with carrying a little bit more of the food, right?" asked Gretchen. "Since I've got this tent?"

"Yeah," said Naomi. "That's cool."

"Nice," Gretchen exclaimed. She looked back down into her stuff and continued. "Lighter. Headlamp. Compass. Map."

"Knock knock," said a voice coming from their bedroom

door. The door was cracked open, and as Gretchen and Naomi turned to see who was speaking, they saw a carefree looking young woman peeking in at them. She had a smile on her face, and when she noticed that she'd been seen, she waved at them.

"Come on in," said Gretchen, standing up from her work and addressing the entering guest. She was skinny and tanned, barefoot, with her thin legs moving up into a short pair of running shorts. The t-shirt she wore was oversized, and didn't look like it belonged to her. Her blonde hair was a bit of a mess, falling out of a bun that had obviously been made in haste.

"Hey there," she said. "I'm Stormy. You guys heading out tomorrow?"

"Yeah," said Gretchen, smiling a bit prouder. "We're leaving tomorrow. I'm Gretchen… or, um, Piggy."

"Piggy," said Stormy, reaching out and shaking her hand. "Nice to meet you."

"I'm Nao—Nova," said Naomi, taking her turn to shake Stormy's hand.

"Nice to meet you, Nova," said Stormy. "You chicks look *fresh*. I bet you're excited to get out there."

"Definitely," Gretchen agreed. "We've been planning this for a while. We just got in this afternoon from Northern Michigan."

"Oh, awesome," said Stormy. "I've camped in the U.P. before. Beautiful up there."

"We're not from that far north," Naomi clarified. "But close."

"Well, I just thought I'd introduce myself and see if you girls needed anything," Stormy went on. "We just finished and we're leaving tomorrow, so if you're missing anything and we might be able to help, let me know."

"Thanks," said Gretchen. "That's nice of you. I think we're looking pretty good here. Anything we should know about the trail?"

"Some hot trail beta?" Stormy said with a laugh.

"Beta?" asked Naomi.

"Just info on the hike," said Stormy. "You know, how it's looking or if there's anything to be made aware of."

"Oh," replied Naomi. "Yeah. Cool. We could definitely use that."

"Well, there's a whole bunch of summer storms moving through lately," said Stormy. "So expect some rain. Sometimes it comes up on you real fast. But hey, it's par for the course for me. That's how I got my name. Whenever I do a hike like this, I get caught in a storm." She laughed again.

"That sucks," said Gretchen. "But I guess if you're out long enough, it's bound to rain."

"No really," said Stormy. "I *literally* get caught in a storm. I was off peeing on our hike, and there I am squatting and it just opens up, pouring rain down on me. What can you do when you've got your shorts down and you're squatting? You just have to finish and get soaked, I guess." Stormy laughed at herself once more. She was obviously a pretty easy-going person.

"Anything else?" Gretchen asked with a smile.

"Pleasant River seemed a bit low," said Stormy. "You

might be able to just rock hop instead of fording it. Oh, and the *mice* are out in full force. Hang everything with food. Like, seriously. Don't even keep a little snack in a pocket of your pack. They will find it and chew a hole. Trust me."

"That's definitely good to know," said Naomi.

"This your first time?" Stormy asked.

"Yeah," said Gretchen. "Both of us."

"Well, I'm not sure how close the two of you are already," said Stormy. "But be prepared to get *close*. Being out there with so little, in the middle of nowhere, hiking *so many miles*, you get friendly with your hiking companions pretty quickly. And don't be afraid to make friends on the trail. Sometimes it's nice to change it up a bit if you're starting to annoy each other. Oh, *and*… really be yourself out there. Have fun and give in to it."

"Thanks," said Naomi.

"Okay," said Stormy, putting her palm up. "I'll let you ladies hike your own hike. We're up and having a few beers if you want to join us. Otherwise, I'll see you when I see you, Piggy and Nova. Peace," she said, flashing the peace sign with her fingers. Without another word, Stormy disappeared through the door.

Gretchen and Naomi looked at one another. They both smiled.

TWO

After a filling, early morning breakfast at the hostel, Gretchen and Naomi along with three other hikers —two men and a woman with English accents—hopped into an extended cab pickup piloted by Bard. It was a quick ride to the trailhead, and the British hikers scurried off quickly. Their plan was to attempt to finish the 100 Mile Wilderness in just five days. Otherwise, they would have to rearrange their flight home. Gretchen and Naomi, however, were taken by a warning sign at the trailhead and asked Bard to take a picture of them next to it.

"Appalachian Trail—Caution," the sign read. "There are no places to obtain supplies or get help until Abol Bridge 100 miles north. Do not attempt this section unless you have a minimum of 10 days supplies and are fully equipped. This is the longest wilderness section of the entire A.T. and its difficulty should not be underestimated. Good hiking!"

"Really puts it in perspective," mused Naomi, considering the sign's warning. "It's like you kind of don't realize what you're truly getting into until it's laid out for you like that."

"You'll be fine," said Bard with a smile. "As the sign says, good hiking!" He smiled and waved at the girls one last time and then walked off toward the van.

"Thanks!" they both called after him.

With their packs tight against their bodies, dressed in long-sleeved technical shirts and shorts, and their reenforced hiking shoes, Gretchen and Naomi set off into the cool and misty morning, beginning their trek into the wilderness.

"No going back now," said Naomi, walking a leisurely pace by Gretchen's side. They had planned for an easy first day to get into their groove, to not burn out too quickly, and Naomi watched Gretchen's gait to match her speed.

"Nope," said Gretchen with a laugh. "This is awesome. Look, beaver dams." Gretchen pointed to the pond they were walking by.

"Oh wow," said Naomi, scoping out the dams. "I feel like I've only seen beaver dams on nature shows." She laughed.

"It's cool," remarked Gretchen. "They're so intricate."

"I'm glad to actually see them in person," Naomi continued. "You ever feel like you watch too much TV and you don't get out and actually *see* things?"

"I did before I moved to Traverse City," Gretchen admitted. "Back when I was in Lansing, working my salary job, my life was a lot of… go to work, come home, eat-TV-sleep, go to work again. I got out as much as I could on the weekends, but it was becoming harder and harder."

"Yeah?" said Naomi. "How was it becoming harder?"

"Well, my friends were becoming less interested in getting out," said Gretchen. "I had done a lot with my roommate at the time, Kim. But then Kim got a boyfriend and went out with him all the time instead. So, eventually, weekends just became time to clean up around the house, run errands, that sort of thing. It felt like I was hardly living."

"I see," said Naomi. "I think that happens to a lot of people."

"I didn't like it," Gretchen went on. "I was going crazy. So I just picked up and left."

"That's super brave of you," Naomi conferred. "I mean, *really*. Not a lot of people will quit their job, leave their home, and move some place completely new without any kind of connection."

"I'm a bit crazy," Gretchen said with a silly grin. "But I'm young. You only live once. Besides, I think the real risk is in *not* doing the things you want. People go all their lives without taking any chances. The end comes sooner than we think. You've got to be you *today*. Tomorrow might not come."

"Yeah," Naomi said with a slow nod, letting Gretchen's words sink in. "Yeah, that makes a lot of sense."

Gretchen let her smile linger, and she reached over and placed her hand on her friend's shoulder. Naomi looked back at her, and she smiled as well.

They passed along Little Wilson Falls, a pretty slate waterfall that looked like a staircase and disappeared into a gully below, and beyond the falls the girls ascended the Big Wilson Cliffs. This was a long section of cliff walking with some impressive views, overlooking a pond, and this stretch culminated at Wilson Stream, a sixty foot wide river that they would have to ford. Standing at the edge of the river, Naomi's face conveyed her trepidation with what they were about to do. Gretchen, although she could feel a sense of anxiety within herself about fording the river, put on a confident face.

"Sixty feet across," said Gretchen. "That's it. Easy peasy."

"Didn't Bard say this might be a tough one?"

"He did," Gretchen replied. "But we've got no choice. Let's get our shoes off."

Together, they removed their shoes and socks and replaced them with their hiking sandals. After another moment of thinking it through, Gretchen enter the stream first. The water felt cool on her bare legs, but very quickly the temperature became mild and warm. She held her shoes together in one hand and began walking, stepping carefully on the riverbed below, trying not to slip.

Naomi watched her friend for a minute and then just went for it. She followed Gretchen into the water and her heart raced as she felt the immediate coolness. The water settled just a couple inches above their knees, but didn't reach the height of their shorts. It took Naomi a few moments of getting used to the sensation of walking through the river, getting her footing, and feeling comfortable with it all, but when she caught on it became much easier than she had imagined.

"This isn't bad," Naomi called out to Gretchen over the sound of the current.

Gretchen looked back at her, smiled wide, and gave her a thumbs up with her free hand.

As Naomi grew even more comfortable still, fording the river with ease, she looked ahead of her and focused her attentions on Gretchen. A new sense of longing filled her heart, something she had never felt before. Previously, she never would have considered walking through a river like this. But Gretchen had inspired her to take this chance, to believe in herself, to try something new. And that inspiration that Gretchen had given her, mixed with the vastness of the landscape that surrounded them, was imbuing Naomi with a reinvigorated sense of love for her friend.

When the girls came out on the other side of the river, they cheered loudly and hugged one another tightly. The sense of accomplishment was palpable, and they both held on to one another for a little longer than one of their hugs might normally last. Once their embrace came to an end, they found a few large rocks to sit on as they put their shoes and socks back on.

"That was incredible," beamed Naomi. "I've never done anything like that. I feel like I'm *glowing*, I'm so happy."

"You are glowing," Gretchen replied joyfully. "I can see it in your face." She reached her hand out and lightly pressed her palm to Naomi's cheek.

"Wow," Naomi said. "Just… *wow.*" She giggled and felt her cheek after Gretchen removed her hand.

"You're giddy," Gretchen said and laughed. "Come on, stand up." Reaching down, Gretchen took Naomi's hands and pulled her up from where she sat.

"Thanks," said Naomi, still feeling that wild energy move through her. For the first time in far too long, Naomi felt an authentic sense of happiness. She had accomplished something she had never thought possible.

Not too far from the river there was a flat clearing, and the two stopped to have lunch. They were only about halfway through the miles for the day and still had a ways to go, but both Gretchen and Naomi felt good. And it felt good to eat. They filled up easily on trail mix—nuts, dried fruit, some chocolate chips—and a few spoons of peanut butter. It wasn't a glamorous meal, but it was calorie-dense and satisfying.

Looking on at Naomi as she pushed a titanium spoon of peanut butter into her mouth, Gretchen couldn't help but smile. Naomi looked so beautiful there with her dark hair woven back in a single braid, her pale face lightly reddened on her nose and just below her eyes, her cheeks filled with peanut butter and trying to get it down. She had removed her long-sleeve shirt as the weather warmed, and sat there in just a tank top and shorts. Seeing her in this environment, under these circumstances, made Gretchen feel all the more attracted to her friend. Her heart ached for Naomi.

"Hey," said Naomi, still trying to swallow a bit of peanut

butter. "Can I get one of those salmon jerky sticks we got from the general store?"

"Oh yeah," Gretchen replied, breaking her adoring gaze on her friend and instead beginning to rifle through her pack. "I'd like one, too."

"Let's eat and walk," Naomi said confidently, standing up and putting her lunch stuff away. "I'm ready to get moving."

Gretchen nodded happily in agreement. And as they set off on the rest of the day's hike, each with a piece of cured salmon in their hand, she felt deep down like something *was* possible here. Something with Naomi. Gretchen wasn't sure how or why she felt it, but it hit her hard. There was a growing certainty replacing the uncertainty of before.

She smiled to herself as she chewed, putting one foot in front of the other. The clouds from earlier had cleared, and the sun was shining down on them. It was a beautiful day in Maine.

Near the end of day one's miles, the girls ended up joining with a group of Appalachian Trail thru-hikers and together they all rock-hopped through Long Pond Stream, the final river of the day. On the other side of the river there was a clearing for tents, and the thru-hikers stopped here to camp, while Gretchen and Naomi pushed further still with plans to sleep in the Long Pond Stream Shelter, just a bit more uphill. Gretchen had checked her phone, and the forecast was calling for rain overnight and they decided together that the shelter would be a better bet.

But as they came upon the shelter, they found that it was already inhabited by a handful of other hikers. In fact, the hikers in question were those very same British hikers that they had started the trail with. There was Queenie, the lone woman of the group, a very freckled redhead, along with her two male compatriots Seb (short for Sebastian) and Cask, who took his name from his love of cask-conditioned beer. They were a delightful and lively bunch, and Naomi found herself loving their accents and the rapport they had with one another.

"The boy won't shut it about his chip butties," barked Queenie with a dramatic eye-roll. "He kept on about spotting a chip shop just over that next ridge."

"It's my comfort food, Queenie," Seb responded sharply, but still in jest. "Pardon if I miss the amenities of home."

"I could certainly eat a donner," mused Cask. "A kebab and a pint, and I'd be right."

Naomi excitedly looked back and forth among these new friends, not quite understanding what they said but enjoying every moment of it. Gretchen caught her looking and smiled.

"Well, it's ramen for us," said Gretchen. "Just too easy to carry and cook." The water in front of her had begun to boil over their camp stove, and Gretchen put her brick of dehydrated noodles into the pot.

"Us as well," confirmed Seb.

"What are chip butties?" Naomi asked, her interest piqued enough that she had to know.

"Oh Lord," Queenie said, dropping her head back.

"Only the most scrumptious sandwich there is," said Seb. "You see, my dear, you take yourself to the chip shop and you purchase your chips—"

"Sorry," interrupted Naomi. "Potato chips?" The Brits all laughed.

"Very cute," said Seb. "But I won't be had so easily."

"No, really," Naomi said, still smiling innocently. "Potato chips?"

"She doesn't know, Seb," said Queenie. "It's not a joke."

"Love," said Seb. "In Britain we call chips what you Americans call French fries. Yeah?"

"Oh God," Naomi replied with embarrassed laughter, putting her hand to her head. "I swear I knew that. Oh my God. I'm sorry. *Jeez*." They all laughed again.

"Have no fear, little Nova," said Cask. "At the recreation outlet, Seb almost popped a bloke for asking if he needed technical pants. My man here thought he was talking about his *smalls*." The Brits all laughed together once again.

"I did not almost pop a bloke," countered Seb. "I knew what he meant."

"You didn't," said Cask, still laughing. "You thought he was criticizing your y-fronts, mate."

"Yeah, well I don't even *wear* y-fronts, now do I *mate*?" Seb boasted. "You know I wear—"

"Knickers," Queenie interrupted. "Seb likes his undergarments frilly."

Gretchen laughed, and she looked over at Naomi, who was wide-eyed with a big silly grin on her face.

"Anyhow," Seb said, putting his hand up. "The conversation at hand. The glorious chip butty."

"Here we go," said Queenie.

"Yes, so… you get yourself to a chip shop, Nova," he went on, miming the story with his hands. "You purchase a bag of chips. Done. You head to your flat, you procure two slices of white bread and you spread butter over each. Chips go in the middle, you make yourself a sandwich, and you enjoy it. It's wonderful. I beg you to try it."

"That's a chip butty?" asked Nova.

"It is," affirmed Seb.

"It sounds… well, I guess it sounds pretty good!" said Nova. Queenie threw her hands up and Cask laughed.

"I assure you, you will love it," said Seb with finality.

Throughout the story, Gretchen had been preparing the ramen for her and Nova. She seasoned it with the small accompanying packet of spice, and made sure to collect all the packaging, fold it up tightly, and push it into a small plastic bag she had for trash. Gretchen handed Nova a spoon, but she was still too enthralled with the conversation to eat. Not eager to wait for dinner, Gretchen began eating.

"I love it," said Nova. "I'm definitely going to try that when I get home."

"You're in for carbo-overload," said Queenie. "Those monstrosities give me such indigestion. I'm feeling ill simply considering it."

"I see now why she's called Piggy," teased Seb. The

group looked over at Gretchen, who was already plowing through the ramen in her pot. Everyone laughed as Gretchen looked up from her meal in surprise.

"Save some for your girl," said Queenie, pointing to Nova. "That one's going to waste away if you don't get some noodles in her."

"That's an oddly sexualized way of describing it," mused Cask. The Brits all laughed and Nova quickly joined in.

"I'm sorry," Gretchen said with embarrassment, pushing the pot away and closer to Nova. "It's *exactly* why I'm called Piggy."

"Don't listen to him, Pigs," Queenie countered. "Seb is afflicted with a congenital case of verbal diarrhea. He gets it from his mum."

"I get it from *your* mum," said Seb.

"She's one in the same!" boomed Queenie.

"Siblings," Cask said quietly, shaking his head.

"Yeah, but she's a bit more like you," Seb continued. "Tough exterior. Mushy exterior. A cunt, through and through."

Nova immediately put her hand to her mouth and looked at Seb. She wasn't sure whether to be appalled or burst out laughing. Reaching over, she put her hand on Piggy's leg for support. Piggy's eyes looked down to Nova's hand, feeling her heart race from the touch, and then she returned her eyes to the conversation.

"I'm sorry," Seb said, putting his hand up in Nova's

direction. "Pardon me. I know we're in mixed company. Brits and Yanks. I'll be more docile."

"Did you really just call your mother *and* your sister a…" said Nova, shaking her head slowly.

"Nova," said Queenie carefully. "In much of the other half of the English-speaking world, cunt is… well, it's more of a term of endearment, really. To be fair to Seb, I am a cunt. And so is our mum."

"Actually, I think you Yanks are missing out," Cask presented. "It's a very satisfying word to say, positive or negatively."

"Okay," Nova said, beginning to come around quickly. She was enchanted by this group, and she couldn't fight their charm.

"Sometimes mates just call each other a cunt in mocking and jest," Queenie further clarified. "It's like two American *bros* might call one another a dick. Or two women call each other a nasty bitch, or something. I don't know all your slang. But it's often friendly."

"It can be used quite negatively, as well," said Seb.

"Oh, surely," Queenie agreed. "It's a keen multitasker, that word."

"It's growing on me," said Nova. "The more I hear you say it."

"We're poisoning America, one impressionable mind at a time," gloated Seb, fist clenched. The whole group laughed.

"What about you, Piggy?" asked Cask. "Coming around?"

"I don't know," Piggy replied with another laugh. "I'll let Nova here throw that word around a bit and see if it sticks."

"We got two!" Seb said triumphantly.

"Don't listen to us, girls," said Queenie. "We're certifi- able. You go on being good. We have enough bad on this side for the lot of us."

After the finer points of language had been discussed a bit further, the group moved on to their well-deserved dinners and even more chatting over a small LED lantern that the Brits had brought with them. Despite the affinity growing between the girls and the Brits, they all had a long day ahead of them tomorrow and the evening came to its natural end fairly quickly after they ate. As the Brits had already claimed the small sleeping shelter as their own, Piggy and Nova hauled their stuff just a little further away and found a clear spot to pitch a tent and put their food up in a tree.

It was a compact two-person tunnel tent, easy enough to haul with them on the hike, but it offered very little space in side for the two of them. As such, Piggy and Nova lay side by side, close and touching, as they settled in for rest that night.

Outside it was quiet, but for the varying sounds of insect life chirping. Nova lay there with a bemused smile and her eyes open as she reflected on the day. She was a bit sore, but she was fine. She felt good.

"Hey," she said softly. "Piggy? You awake?"

"Yeah," replied Piggy quietly.

"Today was awesome," said Nova. "I feel so good about it. About everything."

"Me too," agreed Piggy. Though something about the conversation with the Brits made her feel a little less confident about herself. She couldn't figure out why.

"I loved those English people," Nova continued. "They were so funny and just… bantering and quick."

"Yeah, they're all over the place."

"You think you'll start using the word cunt?" Nova asked, giving Piggy a laugh.

"No," she said, still laughing. "I don't think I will."

"Yeah, me neither," Nova agreed with a smile.

"I think we'd get looked at like we were crazy people if we started throwing that word around," Piggy offered. "Don't you?"

"I think so," said Nova. "But it's kind of charming to think we'd actually get away with it." She laughed at herself, and Piggy smirked in the darkness of the tent. Reaching over, she touched Nova lightly on the side, causing her to reply with a contented sigh.

"Goodnight, Nova."

"Night, Piggy."

THE FOLLOWING MORNING, Piggy and Nova took their time getting going. The Brits had already taken off, as they were a little behind schedule to complete the hike in five days and the girls didn't expect to see them again. Nova was disappointed, hoping that maybe they could all set out together. But she knew their plans.

Breakfast was granola with powdered milk that Piggy reconstituted with water. It was filling and dense, and the perfect way to start their second day on the trail. Before the girls got moving, a group of hikers came through their camp and said hello. They didn't stick around, however, and their eagerness inspired Piggy and Nova to pack up their tent and get hiking themselves.

It was drizzling that morning, and they both put on their lightweight rain jackets as they began an elevation climb up toward Barren Mountain. It took them up over a thousand feet in elevation, amid the alternating mist and rain, aided by some manmade slate staircases on the path. And after another six hundred or so feet of elevation, the girls reached the peak of Barren Mountain, and the old dilapidated lookout tower that was installed there.

They stopped at the summit, and they looked up to the tower. The roof had blown off some time ago, and there was wood debris strewn about on the ground near where they stood. Although they were up high enough for some expected scenic views, the increasingly heavy mist blocked any real visibility.

"Maybe we should climb the tower," Nova offered.

"I don't know," said Piggy. "It looks pretty wet. We might slip."

"Yeah," replied Nova, looking up once again and considering it. "I hope it stops raining."

"At least it's cool," Piggy reconciled. "I mean, if it was

hot and humid *and* rainy, that would be pretty uncomfortable."

"How's the rest of the day looking?"

"For rain or for hiking?" said Piggy.

"Both."

"Um, well," Piggy said, taking out her phone and looking at it. "I'm not getting great reception right now. But when I checked earlier, it looked like it was going to kind of drizzle for much of the day. And for hiking, we've got some rough and steep climbs today. We're going over a few peaks toward Columbus Mountain as well as some peaks that aren't named on the map."

"Okay," Nova said, hefting her pack up onto her back. "Let's get moving, then."

It was a pretty rough day for them. All that mist got them pretty well soaked, and they traversed over many pointless ups and downs, or PUDs as they're called by hikers. It took them a few hours to climb the elevation in front of them, much of it hiked in silence. The first day had been a breeze compared to day two, and Piggy could tell that it was taking its toll on Nova.

Eventually they stopped at a stream to refill their water. They both had their own water filter, a plastic bag that they would fill with water and then attach to a bulbous black filter. Once the filter was secure, they would squeeze the bag and squirt the now-filtered water into their bottles. Piggy also carried a water bladder in her pack, which took some time to fill up. But after a long, wet day of hiking, neither of them wanted to be without water for whatever might lay ahead.

"How high do you think we are?" Nova asked, then pouring a gulp of water into her mouth. Some water dripped down her face and she wiped at it.

"We've done over four thousand feet so far today," replied Piggy. They were sitting on rocks by the stream where they had filled up, and were snacking on trail mix. Piggy took a handful of it, tilted her head back, and dropped it all into her mouth.

"This isn't like yesterday," said Nova woefully.

"It's harder today," Piggy agreed. "Are you going to be okay?"

"Yeah," Nova said, capping her water bottle. "I'll be all right."

"How are your feet?"

"Good," Nova acknowledged. "I don't think I have any blisters yet. How about you?"

"I might be getting one," said Piggy. "But I'm okay."

"I'm feeling a little bit emotional, though," Nova continued. "I kind of feel a little bit like crying."

"Because it's been hard?"

"Yeah, that," she responded. "But it just feels like it's pushing a lot of stuff up inside of me. You know what I mean? Like the difficulty of the hike today has really pushed me emotionally, too."

"Absolutely," said Piggy. "I absolutely know what you mean."

"Sometimes I feel like such a loser," admitted Nova. "I

really get down on myself and I break down. It feels good to cry in those times."

"Yeah, it does," Piggy confirmed. "Why do you feel like a loser?"

"Just because," said Nova. "For many reasons, I guess. I only completed my associate's degree at the community college. And every time I look for jobs to apply to, they all want a bachelor's. But I feel like it's too late for me, or something. To go back and do it."

"It's not too late," Piggy said empathetically. "It's never too late."

"I'm almost thirty," Nova mourned with a shrug. "It would just be weird."

"No it wouldn't," said Piggy, her tone resolute. "You could totally go back and get your bachelor's. People do that every day. Old people. People in their seventies and eighties. I think I read a story about some woman in her nineties going back to school and finishing her degree. You're not a loser for that."

"Thanks," Nova replied with a half-smile. "It's more than all that, too."

"Like what?"

"You know," said Nova. "Still living at home, working at the brewery, not really doing much with myself. I feel this stupid pressure from my family to either do *something* or get married and have a family. I've told you this," she said, and looked down, playing with her fingernail.

"People go at their own pace," said Piggy. "It can take time to find the way you're supposed to go."

"But Gretchen… *Piggy*," Nova corrected. "You left home at eighteen and went to college. You lived away from your family, in the dorms or whatever, and then with friends and on your own. You never went back home after you moved out. I never even moved out."

"I know," said Piggy, her lips flat and her head slowly nodding as she thought about her friend's life in comparison to her own. "We've had different lives."

"I feel so *behind*," Nova admitted with a bit more passion. "That's it, you know? I just want to get on with it. I want to be *free*."

Piggy stood up from where she sat and moved over toward Nova, sitting down directly next to her and putting her arm around her. Nova leaned into Piggy, and although she looked like she was going to cry, she was able to keep her cheeks dry.

"Why don't you feel free?" Piggy asked gently.

"I don't know," huffed Nova. "I just don't."

"It's going to be okay," cooed Piggy, rubbing her hand up and down Nova's back. "You're with me out here in the wilderness. If ever there was a place where you were free, it's here. Look at all this," she said, motioning out toward the stream with her hand. The current flowed at a nice clip, and beyond the stream was a beautiful stand of fir trees. "Pretty, right?"

"It is," Nova agreed solemnly.

"Everything we need, we're carrying with us," Piggy went on. "It's just you and me and nature. We can just be who we are out here with no expectations. You remember that girl we met at the hostel? Stormy?"

"Mm hmm."

"She was giving us some tips, but then she stopped and said she'd let us hike our own hike," said Piggy, "You know what that means?"

"I don't know," admitted Nova.

"It means live and let live, it means accept all kinds," said Piggy. "That's how people operate out here. You let people be themselves and do what they need to do to get it done. Does that make sense?"

"Yeah," said Nova. "It does."

"It means not taking any offense when the Brits start throwing the word cunt around," Piggy said. "I mean, *I'm* not going to start saying it. But that's their world, you know? It is what it is."

"Well, you *did* just say it," Nova teased. Piggy smiled.

"I did," she acquiesced.

"Thank you for being my friend," Nova said, cuddling up against Piggy and holding her. "I don't think I've really had anyone like you in my life." Piggy was still smiling, and that smile grew even bigger and more proud.

"I love you, Nova," said Piggy. "I'm glad we're friends, too. It means a lot to me. You really accepted me when I moved to Traverse City and didn't know anybody. It seems like so many of the locals are off in their own worlds and don't really want to get close with an outsider like me. But you were different."

"I love you, too," Nova replied happily. "You're really special to me."

The girls sat there together on that rock for some time, just embracing one another, happy to be in each other's company. But the break in the rain was coming to an end, and the sky opened up with a light and lazy drizzle, just as it had been doing for much of the day. Reluctantly, they pulled apart and put their hoods over their heads. For a moment, Piggy and Nova stared into each other's eyes, blue into green. Piggy really wanted to lean in and kiss her friend, and so she did. But she craned her neck upwards slightly, and she kissed Nova on the forehead.

"Let's get moving," said Piggy. "We still have more miles to cover before dark."

WHEN PIGGY and Nova arrived in the early evening at the Chairback Gap Shelter, they found that they were the first people to arrive giving them the luxury of hanging their hammocks in the shelter and camping there for the night. In just two days they had gone over twenty-five miles, though only ten of those miles had been hiked on the second day. With the elevation they climbed, the rain, the struggles, it hadn't been a very great day for distance.

After another ramen dinner and a resolution that they would make up their missed miles tomorrow, the girls decided to call it an early night in the hopes that they could get a head start in the morning. They hoisted their food bag up into a nearby tree, making it difficult on any hungry intruders, and ambled with sore feet back into the shelter to climb into their hammocks.

The sun had almost completely set and darkness began to overtake them in the shelter.

"How did your family react to you coming out as gay?" Nova asked, breaking the silence of the impending night. "Did they disown you or call you an abomination or anything like that?"

"No," said Piggy firmly. "They were fine about it, very supportive and happy for me. Happy that I understood myself."

"Are they religious at all?"

"I guess a little," Piggy considered. "I wasn't really raised going to church or anything, but I'd say my parents believe in God or the idea of God or whatever. They don't subscribe to a lot of the negativity that seems to come with Christianity."

Nova was quiet for a few moments, and Piggy wondered what she could be thinking. These questions struck Piggy as very telling, but she didn't want to make any assumptions based on her own biases.

"I'm not sure how my parents would react," Nova said eventually. "I mean, if you had been their daughter and came out to them. My parents are good people, usually understanding and supportive, but it's against their beliefs, you know?"

"Listen," said Piggy. "If you ever need to open up to somebody… you know you can open up to me. Not that you're *not* opening up right now. I'm just saying… that's all."

"I know."

"Have you ever felt attracted to another woman?" Piggy asked bluntly.

"Yes," said Nova.

"Who?"

"I had a friend long ago," Nova began. "Lily French was her name. I haven't seen her in a long time, but we were friends growing up. We spent a lot of time together, in school and in church. I remember one time we had gone downstate for some church concert thing, and Lily and I shared a hotel room. I watched her change before bed, and seeing her in just her underwear made me feel something I'd never really felt before."

"And what was that?"

"Like… *real* arousal," Nova admitted. "I got excited, my heart raced… I got wet."

"So what happened with the two of you?" Piggy said with a delicate tone.

"Later on in high school she got a boyfriend," said Nova. "And then eventually she went off to college down in Holland. We sort of lost touch, especially when I stopped going to church. Before I stopped going, I'd sometimes see her if she was home for a weekend. But when I stopped, I never saw her again."

"I was attracted to girls even before that," Piggy confirmed. "In middle school, I was on the softball team and there was this girl Annie. She was super cute and just naturally good at sports. She ran track, too. Anyway, with her, that was the first time I really found myself thinking about other girls. Some of my friends would start talking about the boys they liked at school, and all I could think about was Annie."

"Did anything happen with you and Annie?" Nova asked.

"Oh no," said Piggy with authority. "No, she was totally into guys. I just had a crush on her, you know? It wasn't until high school that I actually made out with another girl. And then by college…" She just laughed.

"You remind me a lot of Lily in a way," Nova blurted. "You're confident and outgoing. And blonde. She was also blonde."

"Hmm," Piggy intoned.

"I can't believe we're talking about this laying in hammocks in a dark shelter in the middle of nowhere," Nova said through a laugh. "Gosh, it's so crazy that we're out here."

"It's not that crazy," said Piggy. "It's fun, right?"

"It's fun," Nova agreed. "Even though it was a difficult day and I'm tired and I'm sore, I feel really good. I feel like being out here is really good for me."

"I feel the same way," Piggy said. "My feet are feeling a bit tingly now that we're talking about it. But I'm so happy we did this, and I'm so happy you came with me."

"Oh yeah, I was so nervous at first," said Nova. "But now that I'm in it, that's all going away. I feel like I'm really doing something here."

In the middle of Nova's words, a bobbling light flashed into the shelter and put both of them on edge. The light grew closer, and the girls kept silent as they awaited their new arrival. Soon enough, the light was shining inside the shelter, and when it illuminated them in their hammocks, it quickly was pointed down.

"I'm sorry," said a female voice. "I didn't know anybody was in here."

"That's all right," said Piggy. "There's room for another hammock if you want to come in."

"Great," said the woman. They could hear her footsteps on the plank floor under her shoes. She then dropped her bag to the ground and began getting her things ready to store for the evening. It was much too dark to see her face.

"I'm Piggy, by the way."

"Oh, hello Piggy," said the woman. "I'm Quill."

"My name's Nova," Nova joined in.

"Nova," replied Quill. "It's nice to meet you ladies. Give me a moment here while I sling up my hammock."

They gave Quill her space, and she made quick work of her tasks. When she removed her boots, they fell to the ground with a thud and Quill groaned as she pulled herself up into her hammock. She fussed around a bit to get situated and then ended her entire production with a satisfied sigh.

"What a day," Quill spoke eventually into the dark. "Rainy, huh?"

"Very," agreed Piggy.

"You never really get used to the rain and soggy socks," said Quill. "At least, I don't. Are you ladies doing the AT?"

"The entire Appalachian Trail?" Piggy clarified. "No, not this time. Just the 100 Mile Wilderness."

"Well, the 100MW is no *just*," Quill countered. "It's rough."

"Are you all alone?" Nova asked softly.

"Yep," said Quill. "Just me. I'm doing the whole shebang. I'm so close to finished and I can't tell if I'm ready for it, or I'm sad that it's ending."

"Wow," Nova mused. "You're hiking the entire Appalachian Trail by yourself? *How*?"

"Force of will, I guess," Quill said with a laugh. "Also, I'm sort of getting paid to do it. I'm a travel writer and I'm working on a guide."

"Ah," said Piggy. "That's pretty cool. Is that why you're called Quill?"

"Bingo," said Quill.

"Have you done this before?" Nova questioned. "This hike? The AT?"

"I have," Quill replied. "This is my second time. The first time was a few years ago with a group of friends."

"Do you miss being with friends?" asked Piggy.

"Yes and no," said Quill. "I do miss *my* friends, but you meet so many great people out on the trail, you're bound to hook up with groups for stretches. So I haven't hiked the whole thing solo."

"You sound pretty badass," Nova mused, giving Quill a laugh.

"Thanks Nova," she replied. "I guess I am pretty badass. I'd say you girls are badass, as well. Anyone who commits to something like this is badass in my book."

"We're planning to have a big day tomorrow," said Piggy. "Sixteen or seventeen miles. Maybe we could all hike together?"

"I could join you ladies for some in the morning, but I'll have to pick up eventually to hit my pace," said Quill. "I'm shooting for at *least* twenty tomorrow. My plan is to get to the East Branch Shelter by ten or so. I've got to do these hundred miles in five days at most. Hopefully four. I'm not hauling enough food to go much longer than that."

"Okay," said Piggy. "Cool."

"Cool stuff," Quill replied. "All right, I'm going to pass out. We'll chat more in the morning. Goodnight Piggy, goodnight Nova."

"Goodnight Quill," both girls said together.

Then they were all quiet until, just a few minutes later, Quill began to lightly snore. But her snoring wasn't disruptive. It actually felt comforting.

"Goodnight, Nova," Piggy said tenderly through their new roommate's nasally breathing. "I love you."

"I love you, Piggy," Nova shared. "Goodnight."

ALL THREE WOMEN got an early start the next day. And thanks to the morning light, Piggy and Nova got a first look at their new friend. Quill was older than them, probably somewhere in her fifties, with greying hair that she wore back in a bun. She was a rugged and tough looking woman, dressed in khaki shorts, a t-shirt, and a matching khaki vest. On her feet were thick leather hiking boots and high socks. Quill had a kind and beautiful face, aging gracefully thanks to her active lifestyle. She packed lightly, and would often remove a small notebook from her breast pocket to scribble a few thoughts down as they came to her.

They ate a quick breakfast, packed their things, and hit the trail before eight. Piggy and Nova's plan was to get over White Cap Mountain before dusk, though Quill was set on going further than that. But for their opening miles, Quill agreed to give them some company.

"Have you written a lot of travel guides?" Piggy asked as the three of them walked in a group.

"Oh sure," said Quill. "I've done a bunch of work for One Planet, the travel guide publisher."

"Right," Piggy replied with a nod. "I'm familiar with those."

"I mostly prefer to do write-ups on things that are out of the way, hidden gems, hard to get to," said Quill. "Not so much restaurants or tourist attractions. My last big guide was about hiking the PCT."

"What's the PCT?" Nova wondered.

"Pacific Crest Trail," Quill responded. "It's the big one out west. Surely you've heard of it if you girls are up here doing this one."

"Yeah," agreed Nova. "I know it. It was the abbreviation that got me."

"It's over twenty-six hundred miles," said Quill. "Takes five months to do. Longer than the AT. So after doing that guide, I decided to do this one next. That's why I'm hiking it twice. Some people think I'm crazy to do it twice, but I wished I'd done the PCT twice and heck, I've got time."

"I think it's incredible you've hiked so much," said Piggy. "I wish I had the time and money to devote more of myself to it."

"Well, become a travel writer if you want to earn your living doing what you love," Quill said with a short laugh. "But I don't advise mirroring my life history if you want complete freedom of time."

"How did you find the time?" asked Piggy, though she wondered if she would regret her question based on Quill's expression.

"My husband died," replied Quill. "Cancer, about sixteen years ago."

"I'm sorry," Piggy mused solemnly.

"It's all right," Quill said, waving her hand. "We went on a lot of adventures together. We even lived on a sailboat for a year. I like to think I'm carrying the torch, so to speak, by continuing my travels. I do think about him a lot, but I know he would be happy with how I carried on."

"I don't mean to be insensitive," said Nova. "But if you went on adventures a lot with him, how is it that you have more time for adventures now that he's gone?"

"It's not insensitive," Quill said. "When you're in a relationship, even if you're doing this kind of thing together, there's still a lot of compromise. When you're a loner, you're free to come and go as you please. Now, I'd trade it all if it meant having him back. But I'm a realist, I try not to live in the past, and I focus on moving into the future. One step at a time."

Nova nodded slowly.

After going over the summit of Chairback Mountain, the women carefully navigated the scree and talus field on the other side of the slope. Broken rock fragments fallen from the mountain littered the landscape, making it tough to maneuver through in places. Quill advised taking it slow, and putting their hiking poles away in case they needed to use their hands to brace themselves as they descended. The girls followed her sage advice.

Once the talus field ended, Quill informed them that the next stretch was a four mile descent that lead to Katahdin Iron Works Road, an old logging road that she knew to be about thirty miles into the 100 Mile Wilderness. She also let Piggy and Nova know that this was where they would depart.

"It was nice meeting you gals," said Quill with an easy smile. "Watch your ankles in those shoes you've got, and don't forget to drink more water than you think you need. See you around!" Quill waved as they split, her gait growing in speed.

"Goodbye!" they both called back, smiling as well.

"Really cool lady," Nova remarked.

"Yeah," agreed Piggy. "She seems tough as hell."

"Total badass," said Nova.

"Total badass," Piggy repeated.

Quill disappeared pretty quickly after that, as she was much more experienced than Piggy and Nova. But the girls kept on at a good clip, faster than their previous days, which was what they had to do if they wanted to reach Logan Brook by the end of the day. After Quill left, they didn't see any other hikers on their path. It was quiet, but pleasant, and for some time they both just lived in their heads as they pushed further on the trail.

Eventually, after passing the old logging road, they reached the Pleasant River, a rocky stream that they would have to ford. Standing on the west bank, eating trail mix as they watched over the current, they considered the best course of action.

"I don't want to get my shoes wet," said Nova. "We should do it in sandals."

"Yeah," agreed Piggy as she chewed on a mouthful of nuts.

"You know what?" Nova said, looking all around and behind her, seeing that they were all alone. "I feel pretty gross after a few days without a shower. I'm going to take a bath." Squatting down, Nova began looking through her pack for a small bottle of natural and biodegradable liquid castile soap.

"That's not a bad idea," Piggy conferred. Nova was already peeling out of her clothes, all while holding a small bottle in her hands. Piggy then secured her back of trail mix back in her pack and followed Nova's lead.

Without a hint of shame or embarrassment, Nova was quickly naked. And moving into the stream, that flowing water cooling her skin, she carefully traipsed out into the middle of the river where it would be the deepest. Piggy watched her with a curious smile, seeing her ass move up and down with each cautious step. At one point, Nova looked back and gave Piggy a smile. Then she waved to her friend to join her.

Pulling off her own clothes, Piggy followed Nova into the river. At its middle, the river was only about knee-height. But it was deep enough for them to sit down in as though it were a bath. Nova reveled in it with a long, heavy sigh, and she leaned back so as to let the water roll over her head and wet her hair, her breasts peeking out over the current.

"I needed this," mused Nova happily. "It feels incredible. Oh my *God*." Nova was almost moaning, the water felt so good.

"It's great," Piggy concurred, sitting close to her friend in the stream. She took the small bottle of soap from Nova, popped the top, and squirted some into her hands. After handing the bottle back, she stood up, exposing her nude body, and used the soap to begin lathering herself up. Nova remained seated and she watched with a curious smile.

Piggy turned to face Nova as she rubbed the lather through her blonde bush. She grinned.

"Take a picture, it'll last longer," Piggy teased. Nova laughed.

"I left my phone back on the bank," Nova replied. Piggy shrugged.

"Oh well," she said.

Nova then stood up and mirrored Piggy, squirting some

liquid soap into her hands and beginning to wash herself as well. The two of them stood there together, bare and exposed out in the wilderness, just them and nature. There was a slight worry about being caught, about some other hikers approaching the bank and seeing them, but it takes a certain type of person to attempt an adventure like this and that type of person was more likely to join them in a bath than anything else.

Dropping down, Piggy dunked herself back in the water to wash the soap off and Nova soon followed. They splashed up the water onto themselves and rinsed off, both hovering in the stream with their chests exposed. After a few moments, Nova looked up at Piggy, still smiling, and caught Piggy's eyes.

Nova moved closer to her friend, so close that they were almost touching. Then, without another word, Nova leaned in and pressed her lips to Piggy's. It took no prodding at all to get Piggy to return the kiss, and the girls remained there half-submerged in the river for some time, just kissing one another eagerly, with their fingers wrapping around each other's bodies in a handsy embrace.

Once their kiss slowly came to an end, they stared into one another's eyes for some time, just smiling happily and easily. The only sound was the water rushing past them. Then, Piggy stood up, fully revealing herself once more, and she reached a hand down to Nova. Nova accepted it, Piggy pulled her up, and the two walked hand-in-hand back to the river bank to dry off, get dressed, and continue their journey.

ALTHOUGH THE REMAINDER of that day's hike was arduous, the girls took it all in stride and maintained great spirits. Something magical changed after their kiss in the river. Although they didn't really speak about it, question it, try to explain it, the kiss had opened up an entire new dimension of their friendship and their closeness with one another. They touched a lot more on those ensuing miles, they held hands, and they even stopped a few times and kissed again.

Even though they had a slow uphill climb over five miles, taking them up over a thousand feet in elevation, it didn't feel like a slog. Just being together made it easy and enjoyable. It was cloudy overhead, and a subtle mist could be felt as they ascended, but no drizzle could bring them down. Piggy and Nova had found their real connection.

Further on still, tackling another seven or so miles, the girls ascended their way up twenty-five hundred feet of elevation, pressing toward the summit of White Cap Mountain. Piggy revealed that White Cap would be the highest point of their trip, here on day three, and afterwards it would be all downhill from there. This knowledge relieved Nova, and she grinned joyfully. Both of them were having some feet ache issues, but knowing that they would be descending from now on made Nova feel just that much better.

The last mile or so of their climb up White Cap Mountain took almost an hour, but they arrived feeling both accomplished and exhausted just after five in the early evening. The clouds and the mist had cleared during their ascent, while the sun was beginning its own movement down the horizon. Finally reaching the summit, Piggy and Nova dropped their packs to the ground and began to look around.

"Oh my God," said Nova softly, her green eyes wide as they took in the views. From this point where they stood, they could see for hundreds of miles in all directions. They were surrounded on all sides by dense forests and glorious mountain peaks. The sky was enormous and open, some blue peeking through the rollicking clouds. The sun burned deep in the firmament, painting the skyline with various shades of orange and yellow.

"Wait," said Piggy excitedly. She reached into her pocket and pulled out a folded piece of paper. After quickly unfolding it, she looked down into it and read its contents.

Nova was still wide-eyed and blown away by the vastness of all that was in front of her. She looked back and forth between Piggy and the sky.

"Okay," Piggy said, beginning to motion with her hand. "That's south, the way we came. Supposedly we can see two hundred miles of the Appalachian Trail from here."

"Wow," mused Nova, following Piggy's descriptions with her eyes.

"Right here," continued Piggy. "That's Little Spencer Mountain, and Big Spencer Mountain."

"I see 'em," Nova said, eyes focused, offering a nod.

"And there," Piggy said with finality. "That's Mount Katahdin. The highest mountain in Maine. It's name means 'the greatest mountain.' It's over fifty-two hundred feet high and it's the northern terminus of the Appalachian Trail."

"Jeez," replied Nova. It was obvious she was overwhelmed. "Is it the highest point of the AT?"

"No," said Piggy. "That's Clingmans Dome in the Smokies. It's like over six and a half thousand feet, I believe."

"It's so beautiful," mused Nova, changing her views and looking all around her. "It's all so beautiful. This is insane, Piggy. This is just… I can't stand it." Nova began to tear up and she quickly wiped at her eyes. She was completely overcome with emotion.

The world seemed to stretch on forever from their vantage point, a vast natural beauty that was impossible to comprehend. It made Nova feel small and insignificant, but it also made her feel powerful and purposeful and impenetrable. In that moment, she truly was on top of the world.

"It's okay," said Piggy with a caring smile. She moved up closer to Nova and wrapped an arm around her, pulling her in tight. Nova put her own arm around Piggy's back and returned the embrace, resting her head on Piggy's shoulder but not daring to take her eyes off the view.

They stood together for some time, just absorbing everything they could. Nova felt her heart steady and her emotions calm, and a big smile came to her face. After another moment or so, the girls were kissing, pressing firm up against one another, hands gripping to shirts. The kiss was slow and sensual, a meaningful communion that encapsulated everything they had been through so far together.

The sun continued its way down the enormous sky, as Piggy and Nova loved each other on that high mountain top.

After what seemed like a never-ending set of slate stone stairs, the girls hiked together through a stand of birch trees along the path toward their stopping point for the night. It didn't take all that long to arrive at Logan Brook Shelter. On their way in, Piggy and Nova pondered whether or not they might see Quill at the shelter. She very well could have decided to stop early. But when they finally got to the encampment, they discovered they were alone and they just smiled and shrugged.

They decided to pitch the tent for the night, allowing any travelers arriving in the dark to have free use of the shelter itself. The shelter, like the others, was small and looked like a log cabin with a tin roof, one side of the structure completely open. Piggy found a private spot a little distance away from it and began setting the tent up, while Nova broke out the camp stove and started dinner.

Nova took out two vacuum-sealed packages of three-bean chili that they had bought at the general store in Monson, opened them with her pocket knife, and emptied them into their pot. She sauced it up with a little water, and began heating it over the fire. Watching Piggy work on the tent, Nova rested on a rock with her shoes off, and quickly sucked down a small packet of peanut butter as she waited for the chili to come to temperature.

"This is good," moaned Piggy after shoving a spoonful of chili in her mouth. The girls shared the pot between them, as they each dug in with their own spoon. "You never really realize how good food tastes until you hike almost fifty miles in three days." Nova laughed tiredly.

"I'm going to sleep so well tonight," Nova replied. "My legs feel like jelly."

"Are your blisters okay?"

"They're okay," Nova offered. "You kind of get used to it, you know? The pain doesn't always register."

"That's true," agreed Piggy. "Sometimes I just get really tingly in my legs and get focused on that instead of my feet. I guess that's good?" She laughed and shrugged.

"I don't know," Nova said, mirroring her laugh.

"I'm going to eat more than my fair share," Piggy said, pulling back from the pot of chili. "I feel like I'm inhaling it. You eat."

"If you're still hungry, I have another peanut butter packet in my hip belt," Nova said, pointing to her backpack on the ground.

"Great," Piggy said. She stood and moved to Nova's pack, then she leaned down and unzipped the pocket on the hip belt. Piggy came back up with a small white package of peanut butter and she speedily opened it and sucked it down.

"Chili and peanut butter, am I right?" teased Nova. Piggy laughed.

"You never think they'd go together," Piggy said. "Turns out, they do if you burned five thousand calories in a day and you're famished."

"I've never been so hungry," said Nova, spooning another bite of chili into her mouth.

As Nova continued to eat, Piggy went to her own backpack and removed a bundle of paracord. She then moved to a tree and tied one part of the cord to a low branch. Next, she walked ten feet or so to another tree, tied the other end of the paracord there, and tested the tightness. Nova watched as she worked, enjoying her dinner and her moment to relax.

"We should hang up some clothes over night to see if we can dry them out," Piggy advised. "I'm feeling swampy, and if we don't get these clothes dried we might start chaffing."

"Good idea," Nova said, offering a thumbs up.

Piggy then crossed her arms and pulled her shirt up over her head, leaving her standing there in just her shorts and a sports bra. She draped her shirt over the makeshift clothes line and adjusted it so that it wouldn't fall. She smiled satisfied at her work.

After cleaning up the remnants of their dinner, packing their gear away, and hanging their food bag up in a tree, the girls began closing down for the evening. Still nobody had shown up at the shelter and without a care in the world, Piggy and Nova removed their clothes and hung everything they wore, even their socks and underwear, from the paracord clothes line. It had quickly become dark, and with the aid of Piggy's headlamp, they crawled into their small tent and got comfortable.

It was a relief to be naked, as the sweaty clothes had been weighing them down. And inside of the tent, with their sleeping bags open, the girls embraced and slowly kissed one another without saying much at all. Although their feet and legs ached, the affections they gave one another felt like a panacea for all their exhaustion. Soon enough, though, that exhaustion got the better of them, and Piggy and Nova fell asleep, sticky bodies pressed up against one another, cradled in each other's loving arms.

BY DAY FOUR, Piggy and Nova had pretty well acclimated to trail life and the ups and downs it brought them, both literally and figuratively. Although they had already climbed the tallest point of their trip and they would mostly be heading down hill from here, they still had a big climb in Little Boardman Mountain. They hiked downhill for three or four miles at the beginning of their day, hit East Branch Shelter, and then made their way up the mountain.

The day had begun overcast, but it soon cleared up and they got a pretty nice view of the surrounding landscape from atop Little Boardman. Nothing like White Cap Mountain, but out here in the deep wilderness, whenever they got views it was always impressive. On top of Little Boardman, they met a group of thru-hikers doing the AT and found out they had stayed at Logan Brook Shelter the night before, the same shelter the girls camped near. But these hikers had arrived late, left early, and were really pushing their pace. After some pleasantries, the hikers took off while Piggy and Nova lingered for a bit, taking their time.

The early plan for the day was to meet Theo in the resupply van around noon. It was just a mile or two downhill from Little Boardman to get to Kokadjo B Pond Road, where they were told Theo would be waiting. But when they got there, all they found was a desolate, winding, dirty road.

"No service," mused Piggy, staring down into her phone. "What about you?"

"Nope," replied Nova, also holding her phone. After a moment, they both put their phones away as they would be no help.

With their packs on the ground, the girls stood there in silence for a few moments, looking to either side of the road, trying to will the van to arrive with their food.

"I'm sure they'll come soon," said Piggy, trying to stay positive. "They know we're out here and they know we don't have enough food for the second half of the hike."

"How many miles are we supposed to do today?" Nova asked with a tiredness in her voice.

"Twenty," said Piggy. "Are you doing okay?"

"Gretchen, I'm tired," Nova admitted, using Piggy's real name, which she hadn't done in a couple days.

"I know," said Piggy empathetically. "We don't have any more inclines to hike today, it's steady and downhill for the rest of the day. Did you put sunscreen on?"

"I forgot," said Nova.

Piggy nodded and reached down into her pack, removing a tube of sunscreen. Approaching Nova, she squirted a glob of it into her hand and began to rub it into Nova's bare shoulders and arms. Nova smiled gently, her eyes closing, as Piggy rubbed her down.

Then, in the distance, the feint sounds of tires could be

heard rolling and crackling over the dirt road. Nova opened her eyes once more, and together she and Piggy saw a silver van heading their way.

"Yes!" Nova cheered with a clenched fist. "He's here."

When the van pulled up, it had the Hiker Hostel's name written on the side and the girls grew even more excited. Although it had been nice to hike in packs without food weight, they were eager to resupply their stash so that they could get back on the trail.

"Yo," said Theo after stepping out of the driver's side and coming around back. "Gretchen and Naomi?"

"Yes!" the girls said in unison with big grins. They were so happy to see Theo, a gangly hippie guy with dirty-looking dreadlocks, a Hiker Hostel t-shirt, and jeans.

"Awesome," said Theo. He opened the back of the van and pulled a few bags close. "Here's your stuff. How's the hike been?"

"Great," said Piggy as she began rifling through the bags. As she pulled stuff out, food packages that were very similar to what they had brought on the first leg of the trip, she handed it back to Nova. "But we ate the last of our food this morning. We're so happy to see you."

"Nice," Theo replied. "You both look in good spirits. I see a lot of people at this point, and it's not uncommon for the fatigue to really set in. Last week I had a dude ask me to just take him back. I'm glad you girls are pressing on."

"Maybe I'll head back," teased Nova with a weary grin. It was obviously in jest, as her attitude had been revitalized with Theo's arrival.

"We're finishing this thing," countered Piggy. "We're so close."

"Oh, I almost forgot," said Theo, reaching into the van and pulling a cooler closer. He opened the cooler up and produced two cans of light beer and the girls' eyes lit up. When he handed them over to them, the cans felt impossibly cold and they shimmered in the sunlight.

"Oh my God," Piggy said, eyes wide as she looked down at the can in her hand.

"Courtesy of the Hostel," Theo said with a smile. "I'm sure those will taste amazing."

"I feel like I can already taste it," Nova remarked, holding the can up and staring at it.

"Thank you," said Piggy with serious sincerity, looking Theo in the eyes. "This is amazing."

"No sweat," he replied. "If you got everything, I should get moving. I've got to head to Abol Bridge to pick some people up. How far are you trying to make it today?"

"We plan to get to the Antlers campsite by dusk," Piggy said. Both she and Nova had packed all the food they felt they would need, and left a few items in the bags to be send back with Theo.

"That's doable," said Theo. "You're at a real level spot. Shouldn't be hard at all. And the lake at Antlers is beautiful. You'll love it."

"Nice," said Nova. "We could use the break."

"All right, then," said Theo. "I'll probably see you in a few days at the finish line. We're looking at seven at night for the pickup, yeah?"

"That sounds about right," said Piggy. "If we hit any snags, we'll try to call. But we're not getting as good of service out here as some people told us."

"It comes in and out," said Theo. "Let us know if you can." He smiled and waved at them, and then made his way back to the driver's side and got into the van.

"Thank you!" Piggy and Nova called out together, waving at Theo.

"Enjoy the beers!" he replied. With one more smile, Theo started up the van and took off down the dusty road, leaving the girls there, once more, all alone.

Back on the trail, the cold beers were a huge pick-me-up. Never had a cheap light beer tasted so good. Piggy and Nova were both in great spirits, laughing and joking together. The sky was clear now and the sun was shining, and the hiking was as easy as it had ever been on the entire trip. They had each stowed a hiking pole on their packs, hiking now with a pole in one hand and a beer in the other.

The next dozen or so miles were easy, as they both nursed their beers and moved at a steady clip. The stretch they were on was mostly uneventful and flat, but they made the best of it and chatted about life. They had obviously grown much closer to one another over the course of this short but difficult trek, though they hadn't put any labels on what was happening between them. They were simply living in the moment.

"I'm happy about things," Nova said with a newfound confidence. "I'm very fortunate and I shouldn't take that for granted."

"Absolutely," agreed Piggy.

"I know I've got some work to do and I need to figure some life stuff out," she continued. "But that's okay. I just have to start making moves and making decisions."

"What kind of moves?"

"Well, I need to get out of my parents' house," Nova declared. "Even if I'm in the cottage out back, I still rely on them for too much. I think if you and I got an apartment together at Timberline, that would be amazing." Piggy smiled.

"It would," she agreed. "I think we absolutely should do that, when my current lease ends."

"Totally," said Nova. "And after that, I've got to figure out what I'm going to do for work. I can't keep working at Dune City. It's just not enough money to survive and thrive, you know?"

"Oh, I know," said Piggy. "That's why I work two jobs." She paused and thought for a moment. "You might consider doing what I used to do, work as a teller at a credit union. It's full-time, the pay is decent, there are usually good benefits. You don't need a bachelor's degree. And there are so many credit unions in Traverse City, you'll probably be able to get in at one."

"What's the difference between a bank and a credit union?"

"Well," Piggy continued. "A bank is usually for-profit, while credit unions are often not-for-profit or community driven. The idea is that they're a cooperative, and depositors are technically *owners*. Or, well, *members*. Ultimately, they're just more about actually helping people as opposed to a big bank that is really only looking out for itself."

"Huh," Nova replied. "I didn't know that. So you think I could get a job as a teller without a bachelor's degree?"

"Sure," said Piggy enthusiastically. "And it might be a good step for you. You never know where you could move from that position."

"Okay," Nova said, a bright smile moving over her face. "When we get back, I'll apply to work at a credit union and see what happens. I'll definitely give it a try."

"Maybe I'll go back, too," Piggy said, smiling and shrugging.

"Back to Lansing?" said Nova, speaking with a hint of fear.

"Oh no," Piggy corrected. "No, I mean... go back to working at a credit union. I don't know. We'll see."

"Maybe we could work together," beamed Nova, reaching over and putting her hand on Piggy's arm.

"Maybe," Piggy said, still smiling. "Maybe we will."

After a full day of hiking, putting almost twenty miles behind them, Piggy and Nova reached the Antlers campsite just before the sun started to set. After setting up camp on the tip of a peninsula jutting out into the lake, they eagerly pulled their shoes and socks off and waded into the water. The lake felt cool on their aching feet, and the still water seemed to stretch out endlessly. It was one of the more beautiful bodies of water they had seen on their trip.

"I wish I could tear all my clothes off," Nova declared, the water rising just below her knees, her eyes fixed on another group of hikers sauntering into the campsite for the evening. "I could really use a skinny dip."

"Maybe we'll get lucky in the morning," Piggy said with a smile. "And they'll all take off early."

"Think we can have a lazy morning tomorrow?"

"I think so," confirmed Piggy. "By my count, we're right around sixty-three miles for the hike so far."

"You're kidding me!" Nova blurted out, her voice echoing over the lake and she punctuated her surprise with a laugh. "Holy cow. It just doesn't seem real, Piggy. We've already done sixty-three miles?"

"Yep," said Piggy with a grin. "Hard to believe."

"So just thirty-seven left," Nova worked out.

"We're looking at just over eighteen the next two days," Piggy offered. "But I'm thinking they should be relatively easy. We're heading down."

"We're past the midpoint," Nova mused. "I really can't believe it. Never in my *life* could I see myself doing something like this. And here I am, almost done."

"It's amazing what you can accomplish when you put your mind to it," said Piggy. "People do this hike all the time. Why not us?"

"Why not us," Nova repeated with a big smile. In the dwindling sunlight, Nova looked absolutely gorgeous standing there in the water. She wore a tank and her shorts, and her pale skin was now sun kissed and pink on her shoulders and chest. Even her face was getting a bit of color, and the sun made her freckling more prominent. Piggy admired her silently, also wearing a big smile. She wondered what Nova thought about the two of them together. She wondered if Nova felt the same way, or if it was just some sort of trail magic that had injected romance into their adventure.

"Hey," Piggy said softly, reaching out and delicately touching Nova's arm.

"Yeah?"

"What's... going on here?" Piggy asked, putting her cards out on the table. "I mean with us."

"With us?" posited Nova, her face transforming from pure joy to caution and worry.

"Yeah, like..." Piggy begun, averting her eyes for a moment as she tried to put it to words. "Starting with our kiss when we bathed in the river. And everything else that's been happening between us. Sleeping naked together. Kissing. I'm not crazy, right? That all happened."

"Yeah," said Nova with trepidation. She was unsure what to say.

"I guess I was just under the impression that you were straight," Piggy said clearly. She knew inside, however, that Nova's feelings weren't so defined. But she wanted to give Nova the opportunity to speak for herself.

"I don't know," Nova replied, slowly gaining some confidence thanks to Piggy's softness. "I thought I was for a long time, or that I was *supposed* to be. But you know, I've told you things that might indicate otherwise..."

"You've *done* things that might indicate otherwise," Piggy replied with a smile. Nova laughed gently.

"I know," she said. Nova looked down for a moment, kneading her hands together as she worked up the courage to speak further. Soon enough, she looked back up at a smiling Piggy. "Ever since I met you, and I knew you were gay and open about it and happy with your life and doing cool stuff, I was just really inspired by you. And really attracted to you. You're just... you're this amazing woman who knows herself and you're confident and strong in how you live. That's how *I* want to be. When I'm with you, I feel it. And when I'm not, I get scared again. Like I'll never have the kind of life you have."

"Naomi," Piggy said, her lips still forming a happy and empathetic smile. "You're an amazing woman, too. You're caring and kind, and you're thoughtful and enthusiastic. I love being around you. I love working with you at the brewery, and hanging out together around Traverse City. Remember how much fun we had together at the Cherry Festival?" Nova laughed and looked away.

"When I got that barbecue turkey leg that would not stop dripping grease all over my toes," Nova recalled.

"And that ancient guy let us get in his vintage woody station wagon at the car show," Piggy continued. "And he wouldn't stop trying to sell it to us."

"Mm hmm," Nova said with a firm smile and nod.

"Oh, I would kill for one of those turkey legs right now," Piggy said. Nova burst out with a laugh.

"Me too!" she said. "I could so eat one of those."

"What I'm trying to say is..." Piggy rebounded. "This..." she said, motioning between the two of them. "This is something. And whatever it takes to make you feel comfortable with that, I'm on board. I know it's confusing and there may be some difficulty with your family and all that. But I really do love you, Naomi. You're an amazing friend and you mean so much to me."

Nova was still smiling, her happiness apparent on her face. Leaning in, she wrapped her arms around Piggy and the girls hugged tightly. Enveloped in this embrace, wading there just off the bank of that beautiful lake in the middle of the Maine wilderness, surrounded by what felt like almost infinite nature, they both knew that this was right. This was exactly how it was supposed to be.

"I love you, too, Gretchen," Nova said. "Thank you for coming into my life." Pulling back from the hug, Nova leaned in and kissed her friend, and Piggy joyfully returned the kiss. They hung on to one another's arms as they dissolved into the kiss, the sky filled with pinks and purples while the dark orange, glowing sun descended behind them.

After a comforting dinner of pasta with meat sauce, simmered to perfection on top of their camp stove, they moseyed over to where a few other hikers were camping and sat with them around a small fire. They all joked and laughed together, told stories of what their hike had been like so far, and how eager they were to finish it. Piggy and

Nova hung on one another the entire time, holding each other's hand, offering back and forth dialogue when it came time for them to replay their successes and failures, and made it be known to that new group of hikers that they were more than just two friends out on the trail.

To Nova especially, it felt spectacular to be so open physically compared to how she knew she felt emotionally. Her confidence soared, and she was more involved and more vocal than ever. Without a doubt, this trip was changing her at a fundamental level. She knew that for certain. And it made her feel like she could finally be herself. Like there was nothing left to hide.

When the girls ended up in the tent together later that night, they hugged and kissed tenderly until their tiredness got the better of them. It was easy to pass out in each other's arms, and they both smiled warmly as they drifted off to sleep amid the din of crickets and bullfrogs sounding off back and forth in symphony outside their tent.

THE NEXT MORNING, Nova woke up early. She watched Piggy sleep for a few minutes, seeing if she might wake up as well, but eventually Nova decided to quietly shimmy out of the tent and stretch out a bit. Her body was sore, her feet ached, and she knew there was another big mile day ahead of them.

Outside of the tent, the sun was beginning to rise over the lake at the Antlers campsite. There were other tents pitched and a few hammocks slung between trees, but the area where Nova and Piggy had camped, out on a small peninsula, was left to them. The impending sunlight gave the horizon a nice soft orange glow, spreading out over the lake and in direct view of where Nova stood looking east. She smiled to herself, and the pain seemed to melt away.

Nova wore a pair of tight spandex shorts and a sports bra, with her hiking sandals on her feet, and she decided to do the morning routine herself to surprise Piggy. It was usually Piggy's job to lower the food bag and get the coffee going, but Nova was excited to do it herself on this beautiful early morning. Amid the haunting calls of a couple of loons that were occupying the lake, Nova took out the camp stove and she boiled a few cups of water. Once the water was ready, she poured her small stainless steel mug full of hot water, and added to it a thin packet of instant coffee. She stirred it, and then she sipped. The coffee warmed her on this cool morning.

Others around the campsite were getting moving as well. One group had already packed their things and were preparing to start their hiking day. Nova recognized some of these people strewn about. They'd met on the trail, crossed paths, chatted for a bit. Sometimes you would hike past a group, and then you'd stop down the line and they'd overtake you later. There were a lot of great people out here, people with interesting stories and welcoming faces. Nova did wish she had seen the Brits again. Her experience with them was definitely a high point. But most people they had encountered were kind and happy and eager to talk.

Sipping her coffee as she watched the sun rise further up the sky, Nova recalled the previous night and remembered her conversation with Piggy. Or was it with Gretchen? It was with both. They were one in the same, of course. She wondered how things would go from here now that it was all out in the open. In a way, she felt more free than she ever had. But it was still a little scary to be that honest. It had been hard for Nova, harder than it should have been. It made her feel naive—or somehow *behind*—to just now be coming out at her age.

What might have happened, though, if Piggy never came along? Would Nova still be hiding from herself? Would she even *be* Nova at all?

Nova felt an overwhelming sense of gratitude. And watching the sun rise on this new day made it all the better. She was a very fortunate woman, even if she was a little behind in her life. This trip was, in a way, making up for a lot of lost time. Her first time leaving Michigan. Her first time on an airplane. Her first big hike. And admitting out loud to the world that she was gay, even if it only was to an audience of one. That audience was the most important audience, Nova felt. She was sure the rest would fall into place. She hoped so, anyway.

Piggy soon began stirring in the tent, and Nova watched with a smile as her friend crawled out and wiped at her eyes. Lifting herself up off the ground with a groggy smile, Piggy approached Nova dressed in a tank and shorts, barefoot, her blonde hair back in a messy bun.

"The water is still plenty hot," Nova said, still smiling.

Piggy approached her, leaned in, and offered her a good morning kiss. This gesture filled Nova's heart with joy.

"Nice," Piggy replied. She took the pot of water and filled her own mug, and then added the instant coffee just as Nova had earlier.

"The sun rise is beautiful this morning," mused Nova, her eyes looking from the horizon and back to Piggy, who was now taking her first sip of coffee.

"It is," agreed Piggy after her drink. "What time is it?"

"Almost six, I think," Nova replied. "I've been up for about a half hour or so."

"My feet hurt," said Piggy, looking down at her bare feet. "We should soak our feet in the lake before we head out today."

"Good idea," agreed Nova.

"Are you hungry at all?"

"Not yet," said Nova. "My feeding clock is all out of whack."

"I know," said Piggy. "Our timing seems different every day. And last night's dinner was pretty filling."

"I'm feeling good, though," admitted Nova. "Even though I'm in a bit of pain, I feel like I've got a lot of energy."

"Think you can do eighteen miles today?" Piggy asked with a sly grin.

"Definitely," said Nova. "I feel like I can do anything."

"That's the spirit," said Piggy happily. "I like to hear that."

"What about you?"

"I can do eighteen," Piggy confirmed with confidence. "Absolutely. We're in the home stretch. We are almost *done* hiking the 100 Mile Wilderness. It's been a dream of mine forever."

Nova just smiled and took a drink of coffee.

"You know," Piggy continued. "I'm really proud of you."

"Yeah?" Nova said with a new light in her eyes.

"Yeah," said Piggy. "For you to even come out here and do this hike, that took a lot of guts. I've at least done a few shorter in-and-out hikes and camping, gone for a few days at a time, so I had some idea of what to expect. But you've never really done anything like this."

"No, I haven't," said Nova.

"And you're doing great," Piggy conferred. "You're pushing through, no injuries, limited whining." She winked and Nova laughed.

"I've tried to keep my whining to a minimum," Nova teased.

"You have," said Piggy smiling. "But even greater than all that, even bigger than you taking on such a tough hike, you did one of the toughest things of all. Last night. You really expressed yourself, and I know that was really hard for you. But I'm here, by your side, and you don't have to do this alone." Reaching out, Piggy took Nova's hand and squeezed it affectionately.

"I'm so happy for that," said Nova, squeezing back. "I'm going to need your support and confidence once we get back home. I worry a little bit that I'll have a harder time back there."

"I know," Piggy said tenderly. "And I'll be there for you."

The girls kissed once again, slowly and delicately. Being together, it just felt right. Nova knew that it was Piggy she wanted to be with, and she was so relieved that she could finally admit that to herself.

Piggy and Nova spent the morning lazily preparing for their day. They had another cup of coffee, split a piece of salami and ate some trail mix, hit the privies at the campsite, and then began collapsing their camp and getting ready to leave. Once they were all packed up, they spent some time sitting on rocks near the lake, soaking their sore feet, and talking about the plan for the day's hike. It would take them by Pemadumcook Lake, along Nahmakanta Stream, and to Nahmakanta Lake. Further still, they would make an ascent up Nesuntabunt Mountain, though it wouldn't be too steep, Piggy confirmed. Finally, they would end at Crescent Pond if all went well. By Piggy's calculations, those eighteen miles should take them nine hours.

By the time they had their packs hoisted up on their backs, the girls were lively and excited, feeling chatty and enthusiastic for the day. Their feet were dry, socks and shoes secure, and they left no trace that they had camped in the spot they did. Nearing nine in the morning now, they were some of the last hikers to leave the campsite and hit the trail. But they were happy to have had a leisurely morning together. It filled them with energy and joy, and as they began their hike out, they held hands tightly and left the campsite as one.

Even though this trip was in honor of Piggy's thirtieth birthday, her own ascent into a new decade of life, Nova felt like she was the one who was gaining the most from the experience. In fact, she felt like a new woman. She felt the change was powerful and important. Being out in the deep wilderness was so freeing, and the freedom she now felt was unlike anything she'd ever felt before. It was transcendent.

UPON STOPPING to take in the views atop Nesuntabunt Mountain, including a very nice view of a much closer Katahdin on the horizon, Piggy and Nova noticed another hiker approaching from behind. They turned to address him with smiles and hellos, and as he walked closer he stopped and greeted them as well. He was a lithe man, of an indeterminate age—he looked young, but he very well could have been in his forties. He wore a lightweight linen pullover shirt in a natural ecru color, and bright red and very short running shorts. On his head was a wide-brimmed straw hat, and black plastic sunglasses.

But the most interesting thing that the girls noticed upon seeing him was that his backpack was much smaller than theirs, perhaps even half the capacity.

"Guru," he said humbly, as he shook their hands and they exchanged names. "I know it sounds pretentious, but I didn't choose it." Piggy and Nova laughed.

"What is the deal with this pack you've got on?" Piggy asked. "How could you possibly carry everything you need in there?"

"Oh, I'm doing this trail in two days," Guru declared simply. When they heard this, both girls exclaimed.

"What!" Nova said. "You couldn't possibly…"

"Yeah, it's just practice for a race I'm running next month in Colorado," said Guru. "I'm an ultramarathon runner."

"You're kidding," mused Piggy. "*Two days*?"

"Two days," Guru confirmed. "I'm not stopping in the night to sleep, just pushing through. I'll probably finish around midnight tonight, or earlier if I don't stop to talk to people." He grinned.

"Well, we're heading down to Crescent Pond to stop at the campsite there," said Nova. "Do you want to walk with us for a bit?"

"Sure," he said. "I could use the company."

Piggy and Nova picked their packs up and put them on, and now with a third member of their party, they began the descent down the mountain and toward camp.

"The race I'm doing is called Run Rabbit Run," Guru said as the three of them walked together. "It's a hundred miles through Routt National Forest in northern Colorado. The elevations are much steeper out there. I'm looking at around twenty-one thousand feet of total climbing in that one."

"That sounds absolutely insane," barked Nova. "What kind of time do you expect?"

"Oh, I really don't know," Guru replied. "Better than the two days I'm doing here. This has ended up as more of a leisurely pace because you encounter so many people who want to chat, and it's hard for me to say no to that kind of friendliness. People won't be chatting during the race."

"What's a *good* time for an ultramarathon?" asked Piggy.

"For that particular race," said Guru. "About eighteen hours." Again, the girls were blown away. "But I don't expect that kind of time. I'm relatively new to ultramarathoning. I'm hoping more like thirty hours. But we'll see."

"Okay, so I've got to know," said Nova. "How did you get the name Guru and does it relate to this ultramarathon running?"

"Sort of," admitted Guru. "It comes more from the one-eighty I did in life. Some of my extreme sports friends started calling me that after they learned my history."

"And that history is… ?" Piggy prodded with an eager smile. Guru smiled back.

"Well, in my previous life I was a pretty sedentary guy," he began. "I worked in software sales in Boston. Ended up out of shape, tired all the time, just working this job because it paid well and cost of living in Boston was high. I got fed up with all that, but I didn't know of a way out. I tried to talk to my wife about it, but she just kept pushing me to stay at my job, stay on the treadmill, all that."

The girls listened intently to Guru's story, their eyes only moving from his face occasionally to scan the trail in front of them for any obstacles that might be coming.

"At the time, I had a hard time admitting to it," Guru

went on. "But I was feeling suicidal. And I read somewhere that any time you feel like that, it's your body telling you that you need a change. My wife thought I needed pills. Fast forward a bit and I found running, then ultra-running, mixed with a massive amount of downsizing in my life. First I started getting rid of most things that I owned, then the job, and soon after that my wife left me because she thought I'd gone bananas."

"Sounds like a catch," Nova grumbled, giving Guru a laugh.

"She has her own flaws she's working through," he said. "I don't fault her for it. We became incompatible. I was no longer the man she thought she had married. But through all of this… through this shedding of my old skin, I've begun to find my place. Currently I live out of a Class C RV and travel all over for running. It's been a tremendous blessing."

"Wow," said Piggy. "That's some story. You're feeling good, though?"

"I'm feeling great," said Guru. "Never better. I feel like I'm finding myself out here, really and truly. That old life wasn't me and it didn't make me happy. This is where I'm supposed to be."

"I can't believe you fit everything into a small RV," said Nova. "You really live out of it? You don't have an apartment somewhere? Or a storage unit?"

"Nope," Guru confirmed. "No apartment, no storage unit. Everything I own is in that RV, and truthfully… it's very little. I've got my clothing and gear, and a small laptop, and…" he paused in his words as he thought about his possessions for a moment.

"That's it?" asked Nova.

"I'm trying to think," said Guru. "I mean, there's a few kitchen items in there. But it's really just clothing and my computer. I guess I constructed my life so that if I go back to where I parked my RV after this hike, and the RV has been stolen, I won't really miss much."

"Damn," said Nova. She slowly nodded her head as she let it sink in.

"That's why they call me Guru, I guess," he said. "I kind of live this minimalist, almost ascetic lifestyle. And ever since I escaped that dark time in my life, I've felt pretty consistently happy."

"I think that's awesome," said Piggy. "It seems like you've got some stuff really figured out."

"I think I do," Guru conferred. "At least, for *me*. Your mileage may vary, of course. I don't advise everyone just chuck it all and start running ultramarathons."

"Okay, so…" Nova posited. "What *would* you advise? I mean, what kind of advice would you give someone who felt a little lost and out of place, like you did?" Piggy looked over at Nova, who knew exactly where Piggy's question was coming from.

"I would say… *to thine own self be true*," Guru quoted. "People can interpret that in many ways, but I think the way it was meant by Shakespeare at the time and in that particular scene of *Hamlet* was you have to look out for yourself first and foremost. You can't help others if you can't help yourself. You can't *love* others if you can't love yourself. It's not selfish to take care of yourself, to love yourself, to do good by yourself. You've got to be you, even if it upsets or disappoints others. Because you're doing everybody a greater disservice, including yourself, if you're faking it or living a false life."

Guru paused for a moment and looked skyward. Then a smile curled over his lips.

"Yeah," he said with finality. "I think that all sounds right."

"Thank you," Nova said, feeling weightless and buoyant, letting Guru's words sink in. "That makes a lot of sense."

"I hope so," replied Guru. "Hey. This must be Crescent Pond we're coming upon and I should really pick up the pace if I want to finish by midnight. Lovely meeting you two, and I wish you all the best in your hike."

"Thanks," Piggy said with an easy smile. "It was nice meeting you."

"Nice meeting you," Nova agreed. "And thanks again for the words of wisdom. I see why they call you Guru."

"Yeah," said Guru, waving his hand with a hint of embarrassment. "I act like a fool when I'm drunk, just like everyone else. Take it easy!" With that, Guru's pace increased and he very quickly broke away from Piggy and Nova. Soon enough, his pace was a steady run and he disappeared around a turn in the trail.

Piggy and Nova hiked together for a few moments in silence as they considered what Guru had said. To Nova, he had made a lot of sense and he only reenforced the kind of thoughts she had been having for some time. But his advice also hit home for Piggy, as well. She found herself meditating on Guru's nomadic lifestyle, as it was something she had considered in the past. It was enticing, surely, but there was also something lonely about it that Piggy just couldn't see herself enduring.

The Crescent Pond campsite was now in front of them, and although they looked around for Guru he was nowhere to be found. Locating a comfortable spot at the site and taking off their packs, the girls began settling in for yet another night of camping. They sat together as they ate dinner, they kissed, and they spoke of what the following day —the last day of the hike and Piggy's birthday—might entail. It was exciting and energizing, and it was all turning out to be something far greater than either had expected.

WHEN PIGGY OPENED HER EYES, a sleep-tired smile on her face, she found the tent unzipped, the early morning sunlight shining in, and no Nova next to her. She squirmed a bit, feeling the tightness in her calves that she knew would subside after a mile or so of hiking, and she tried to remember where she had last put her bottle of aspirin. Then it hit her. There was an aroma in the air, something she knew well but just couldn't place, something flavorful and tasty. Piggy's mouth began to water and she quickly shimmied out of the tent and into the light outside.

And that's where she found Nova, grinning as she

worked over the camp stove and a small skillet. Nova was cooking something good, something that seemed so far removed from what they had been eating for the last week. The smell was so good, Piggy almost thought she was dreaming.

"What is that?" she remarked as she closed in on Nova.

"Happy birthday!" Nova called out with a smile, lifting a spatula in the air. "We're having a bacon and cheese omelette for breakfast."

"What?" Piggy said, still in shock. "*How*?"

"How what?"

"How did you get any of that?" asked Piggy. "Bacon? Cheese? *Eggs*?"

"See that group of hikers over there?" said Nova, pointing with the spatula across the campsite. "I sold my body to them in exchange for all this."

"Nova!" protested Piggy, giving Nova a big laugh.

"Just kidding," Nova continued, still grinning. "They're reverse hiking the 100 Mile Wilderness," she clarified. "It's their second day, and they found out they were a little overzealous in their packing. They had a few eggs break yesterday in one of their packs, and they just wanted to use them up. So I traded some of our extra packaged food for their eggs. They also gave me some cheese. And the bacon is just bacon bits, but it does the trick!"

"That's amazing!" said Piggy. "It all smells so good."

"It's your birthday breakfast," Nova beamed. "You're thirty!"

"I'm thirty," Piggy replied with a laugh. "And I'm hungry."

"Well, I've got some warm coffee for you," said Nova. "Grab your mug, have a seat on that log, and get ready for the best omelette you've ever eaten."

"Gladly," said Piggy. She still couldn't tell if she was dreaming, but if she was, Piggy only wanted to wake up *after* eating.

The girls ate together on the log, looking out at Crescent Pond in the growing light of the rising sun. The omelette really was the best one Piggy had ever eaten. That was probably because it was their sixth day on the trail and it was the freshest, most home-cooked style food they had had. But also because it was made with love by Nova. Nova smiled as she watched Piggy eat, and it was obvious from the looks on their faces that the two had fallen hard for each other out there in the wilderness.

They happily packed up their camp for the last time of the trip, their spirits high, and their energy rising. After returning the skillet and spatula to the group Nova had borrowed it from, and sharing with them a little trail knowledge, the girls once more donned their packs and hit the road. It was a beautifully clear morning, with a nice crispness in the air that they knew would soon give way to the summer heat. But they felt good, ready to tackle their last day on the trail.

The miles and the hours flew by easily. There was a bit of a climb up Rainbow Ledges, but the view of Katahdin framed between pine trees they received made it worth the ascent. They talked of the logistics of getting back home, and how eager they both were to return to civilization. And they also talked about what kind of adventure they might go on for Nova's thirtieth birthday, just a few months down the line.

The final six miles of their hike was downhill and easy. It was probably a mix of adrenaline and an eagerness to finish the hike that gave Piggy and Nova their energy. The day had been a happy blur, and by the time the sun was starting to begin its descent, they finally emerged from the woods and came upon a road. Their welcome back to civilization was from a big logging truck flying by.

"So where do we go from here?" Nova asked, looking left to right on the paved road.

"Well," Piggy said, taking out a map. "This is Golden Road. So I think we just walk a little ways down here and we should get to Abol Bridge."

"All right," said Nova, taking a deep breath and holding tightly to her backpack. "Let's soldier on."

"This way," Piggy said, motioning with a finger.

Not long after, they indeed came upon Abol Bridge, spanning across the Penobscot River. Off in the distance was Mount Katahdin once again, towering over them and closer than ever. It almost didn't seem real that this was the end, and they both lamented that they weren't actually continuing on to Katahdin and climbing to its summit. But as they traversed Abol Bridge, the river rushing underneath them, it was obvious that they had left the deep wilderness. A white van towing rafting tubes sped by them, possibly heading to the very same campground they were headed for.

There was no fanfare as they ambled into the Abol Bridge Campground, though one might expect streamers and noisemakers and a fistful of cake after hiking a hundred miles in the remote woods. Piggy joked that she might have paid extra had they been greeted as such, though Nova mused that eating cake might make her throw up after such a strenuous week. There was a general store in the campground, and that was where they were to meet whoever was picking them up from the Hiker Hostel. But seeing as they had arrived before the van, they went into the store to see what they had to offer.

It was closing in on seven, and it was starting to get dark. As Piggy and Nova sipped a couple of beers they had bought from the store, they waited on a picnic table for their ride to arrive. They sat in silence, the tiredness finally beginning to set in. Still cradling her beer in one hand, Nova reached out for Piggy, and Piggy took her hand. Their silence continued, as the cold beer rejuvenated them and brought them back to reality.

Just a few minutes after seven, that familiar silver van rolled up to the now closed general store and the girls' eyes lit up. They both bolted upright from their seats and grabbed their packs, tossing their empty beer cans into a recycle bin and then speed-walked over to their ride home.

Stepping out of the driver's side was a short woman, a woman they quickly recognized as Chickie. She greeted them with a tender smile.

"I hope I'm not late," Chickie said with empathy. "How long have you ladies been waiting?"

"Just a half hour or so," said Piggy. "You're fine. Not late at all."

"Oh good," said Chickie. "So how was it? Everything you had hoped?"

The girls looked to one another and smiled warmly.

"Definitely," said Nova.

"It was intense," said Piggy. "But amazing. I can't believe it's over."

"It's too bad we're not pushing on to Katahdin," said Nova. Piggy laughed.

"Oh, do you want to?" Chickie asked. "Do you have enough food?"

"No!" said Piggy, laughing once again. "We're done."

"Yeah, I think we're done," Nova agreed with relief.

"Well, you're my only pickup," said Chickie. "So whenever you're ready." She opened the side door of the van, and the girls began loading in.

"How long does it take to get back to Monson?" Piggy asked after tossing her pack in the back of the van.

"About two hours," Chickie revealed.

"Wow," mused Piggy. "Two hours. It took us six days."

"We've got hot showers back at the hostel just waiting to rejuvenate you," Chickie said, standing to the side as both Piggy and Nova now climbed in and took their seats. "Feel free to sleep on the ride if you like. I'm pretty deep into a podcast I'm listening to." She laughed at herself.

"Yeah, I could use a nap," remarked Nova. She locked her seatbelt and kicked out of her sandals.

"I could sleep for a week," said Piggy.

"Buckle up," Chickie said, now slamming the van door closed and walking around to the driver's side.

The ride back was comfortable and relaxing, the road flanked by the very wilderness that the girls had just spent so long making their way through. The lull of the drive mixed with the gentle timbre of the voices on Chickie's podcast quickly put both Piggy and Nova to sleep. They rested easy in their sense of accomplishment. They had tackled a hike that very few people dared. And on the other side of that hike, they were both permanently changed. They were now truly adventurers and risk-takers, women who lived life with vim and vigor.

Nova's head rested on Piggy's shoulder. They were both smiling in their slumber.

When they got back to the Hiker Hostel, Piggy and Nova immediately hit the showers in separate bathrooms just down the hall from each other. It was closing in on ten at night, and the hostel was mostly quiet. The girls stepped out of their respective bathrooms at the same time and met up in the hallway, both of them smiling wide and looking refreshed, dressed in more casual shorts and shirts that they had left with their duffel in a locker.

"That was the best shower of my life," Piggy said,

running her hand overtop of her damp hair. "I feel like a million bucks."

"Oh my God," Nova exclaimed. "Magic. Just absolute magic. I almost feel like I could go hike another hundred miles." They both laughed.

"Yeah," said Piggy skeptically. "I think I'll leave you to it."

"You have to come with me," Nova replied, keeping her tease going. "I only want to go back out there if you're with me."

"Okay," Piggy said, now leaning in and planting a sweet kiss on Nova's lips. "Let's get our backpacks on and head out." Nova laughed and then she pushed up against Piggy, giving her a big, loving hug.

For a moment, they discussed heading outside to sit by a bonfire with a few other people who were in the backyard. But they decided against it. They had, after all, just spent six full days outdoors, and it felt much more comfortable to be back inside with running water, and walls, and a bed. They shut the door behind them as they entered their bedroom and after ditching their dirty clothes and bathroom items, they ended up in one of the two beds together.

"I almost don't want to go home," said Nova, speaking between kisses as she and Piggy lounged with one another. "I'm not ready to go back to reality."

"Why not?" Piggy asked, punctuating her question with another kiss.

"I'm just not," Nova replied, a subtle malaise moving over her.

"Hey," said Piggy empathetically. "Don't worry about things. You just did something incredible. You're a total beast. If you can do a hundred mile hike, you can do anything."

"Yeah?" Nova replied. She paused, and then she smiled. "Yeah, you're right."

"Of course I'm right," said Piggy. "When we get home, things are going to change for you. For us. And for the better. I promise."

"I sure hope so," Nova mused.

Nova's plaintive wishing soon dissolved into more kissing, and the two of them ended up lying down next to one another on the bed, in each other's arms, exploring each other's tired bodies with eager hands. It all came naturally for Nova, and as they grew more fervent and impassioned, she felt something switch inside of her. At first, this was just an indolent make out session with her best friend, but it suddenly dawned on Nova that she was lying in bed, kissing and groping her new lover.

Piggy began tugging on Nova's shorts, trying to pull them down over her ass, and Nova felt her heart begin to race.

"Take these off," Piggy implored softly, as her lips moved from Nova's lips down to her neck.

"My shorts?"

"Mm hmm."

"Okay," Nova said, her heart throbbing more still. She pushed her hands into the elastic band of her shorts and guided them down her hips and along her legs. Underneath, she wasn't wearing anything else.

Piggy sat up a bit and helped her, grabbing for the shorts and taking them off of Nova's feet, tossing them aside. Then, sitting on her knees on the bed, Piggy reached down to her own t-shirt and pulled it up over her head. Her pale breasts tumbled out, showing off her noticeable tan lines. Nova then excitedly scrambled, and she removed her shirt just as Piggy slipped out of her shorts. Both of them were more than eager to get naked for one another.

"You're so hot, Piggy," intoned Nova, looking her up and down. "You're beautiful."

"Thank you," Piggy replied with a grin. "And I should extend the compliment back to you. I think you're absolutely gorgeous."

Nova smiled and blushed, shying back a bit. But she loved the attention. And she loved Piggy.

"You've never had a girl go down on you before, have you?" Piggy said, her hand rubbing up and down Nova's thigh.

"Nope."

"Well, you're in for a treat," Piggy said with an excited sparkle in her blue eyes. Leaning in, she placed a single, delicate kiss on Nova's pussy lips. "We're actually *good* at it."

Nova laughed and covered her eyes for a moment in a tickled embarrassment. But it was all just a cover for her burning red excitement. It felt like her heart was about to rip out of her chest. And when she felt Piggy dive in, releasing her tongue and pushing it firmly through Nova's lips, it all became very real. Letting out a low, achy moan, Nova uncovered her eyes and stared down the length of her own body, watching Piggy eat her out.

And immediately Nova found Piggy's words to ring true. She had a few lovers over the course of her young life, but none of them women and none of them as good as Piggy at her current charge. Piggy licked up and down slowly, enjoying and reveling in the act. She parted Nova's lips with her fingers and licked deeper still, until she found Nova's clit and offered it her attentions. Wrapping her mouth around it, Piggy lightly sucked as her tongue flicked back and forth on Nova's pink little on-switch.

"Oh my God," Nova let ooze out of her mouth, pressing a hand to her now sweaty chest. "That's so good, Piggy. That's so good."

"Mmm," hummed Piggy, pulling back for a moment and looking up to Nova, as she rubbed her fingers back and forth over her lover's wet flesh. "Makes you forget all about the foot pain, huh?"

"What?" said Nova, as though she had no idea what Piggy was even talking about. Piggy just laughed and leaned back down, attacking Nova's pussy with a revitalized sense of desire. Nova dropped her head back and moaned once again.

Nova felt her temperature rising, along with her arousal. What was happening between her legs was a dream come true, something she had always imagined but never acted on. And now this was her real life. This was exactly what she wanted, had forever wanted, and there would be no going back. Opening her eyes, she watched Piggy work. Her blonde hair framing her beautiful tan face, Piggy's own eyes were closed but her mouth was open and her tongue was loose. Nova watched Piggy lick her, and never had she felt more loved in her life.

Without warning, something changed inside of Nova and her excitement increased tenfold. Her breathing got heavy, and she could feel her toes beginning to twinkle. Propped up on her elbows now, she couldn't take her eyes off of Piggy. And Piggy, still lapping up Nova's sex, looked upward for a moment only to see the intense longing on Nova's face. It was obvious that she had unlocked the passion deep inside of Nova.

"Oh God," said Nova with a shortness of breath, her eyes unmoving and watching her lover. "Oh God, I'm close. I'm so close. Piggy, I'm almost there. Don't stop."

Piggy obeyed. And then Nova started to convulse and squirm, still trying to hold herself up on her elbow. She was coming, but Piggy did not stop nor did Nova want her to. The orgasm tore through her with fury and flame and it felt transcendent. Nova felt like she was on some higher plane of existence. She kept her focus and she felt every bolt of energy her climax offered.

"Oh!" Nova called out, finally succumbing to the pleasure. She fell over to her side and balled up, wrapping her arms around herself as she felt a cold sweat coming on. Piggy meanwhile, a big grin on her wet face, popped up from the bed and rested on her knees, sitting next to Nova and delicately petting her thigh.

"Wow," said Piggy, looking down at Nova with pure adoration in her eyes. "You came really hard."

"I did," agreed Nova with a low whine, her eyes closed, still holding herself. Piggy laughed.

"Your hair is kind of a mess," teased Piggy, fluffing up Nova's shower-damp hair.

"I don't care," Nova replied. "You can tie it in knots for all I care." Piggy laughed once again.

"I would never do that to you," Piggy said, her face glowing, still admiring Nova. "I love you too much to ever do something so evil."

Nova smiled at Piggy's words. Slowly, she opened her eyes and released herself from her own embrace. Rolling over onto her back once again, she looked up at Piggy.

"I love you, too," she said. "This has been the best trip of my entire life. Thank you so much. Thank you from the bottom of my heart. And happy birthday." Piggy smiled and offered a small laugh.

"Oh yeah," replied Piggy. "It's my birthday, isn't it?"

"Mm hmm."

"Well, I think I got the best birthday present ever," Piggy said. "You."

Joy washed over Nova's face. As she came down from the clouds, her gaze focused on Piggy, she wished for this night to never come to an end. The exhaustion of that hundred mile hike had been wiped away with the sense of accomplishment she felt for completing it. And now the feeling of love brewing inside of her for Piggy was unlike anything she had ever felt before. It was a powerful moment for Nova, and she wanted to hold on to it forever. It felt like the dawning of a brand new life for her.

And Piggy felt it, too. The love she felt for her friend—and now most certainly her lover—was more than she'd felt for any other woman. She had adored and craved Nova upon the first time meeting her, but she felt off limits. Now that the two were intimate, and growing closer with each passing moment, Piggy felt as though she were now walking the path to true love. There was something in Nova's eyes when Piggy stared into them. There was some sort of joint connection, something unspoken, in their hearts.

This had been the greatest adventure of both of their lives. And no doubt would things be even better once they got back home.

THREE

When they did return home to Traverse City, Gretchen soon felt things had gotten a little weird. Although Naomi was just as animated and excited as Gretchen when she recounted their trip to some of the regulars at Dune City, she shrugged off some of Gretchen's more affectionate attention in public. And after an entire week of being back, Gretchen was beginning to worry as Naomi didn't appear that interested in hanging out outside of work at all. It was almost as though whatever had happened between them on the hike hadn't really happened.

It felt so distant, that Gretchen actually questioned if it *did* happen. Maybe she had imagined it, or maybe even blown it up to more than it actually was. But Gretchen and Naomi *did* have sex that last night at the Hiker Hostel, Gretchen was positive. She wasn't imagining things. So why would Naomi pretend like it didn't happen? Why wouldn't she jump into this feet first?

Gretchen knew that she had to get Naomi to talk about it. And that couldn't happen at work. One thing that carried over from their trip was Naomi's newfound interest in applying to jobs at a local credit union, so Gretchen approached her to ask if she wanted to get together to talk about that. Naomi happily agreed.

They met up at a cafe downtown on Front Street at Naomi's insistence. Gretchen had hoped for something more private, but at that point she was ready to take what she could get. Late summer in Traverse City was busy with tourists, and a constant stream of people entered the cafe, placed their order, and left. Gretchen and Naomi sat in the back at a small table, each of them with a laptop open in front of them.

"Now this is interesting," said Gretchen. "It looks like *my* old credit union is opening two branches up here in Traverse City. I can't believe it."

"Whoa, really?" Naomi replied. "Send me the link."

"All right," Gretchen agreed. She tapped some into her keyboard, texting the link over to Naomi. "It looks like they're starting to hire for jobs shortly."

"And they're a good company to work for?"

"Yeah, absolutely," confirmed Gretchen. "I was generally happy there. It was just my own issues that made me leave."

"Do you think you would be able to write me some kind

of letter of recommendation?" asked Naomi. "Or would that not even matter?"

"I think it would matter," Gretchen said. "And yes, of course I would do that for you." She smiled plainly, with much more on her mind than just the conversation at hand.

"Thank you," Naomi beamed happily. "I'm going to start this application process right now."

"Hey," said Gretchen. "Before you do…"

"Yeah?" Naomi said, her eyes now focused on her computer screen.

"No, hey, look up," Gretchen implored. Naomi looked up.

"What?"

"Listen, things have felt weird ever since we got back from our trip," she said. "I don't know if you've felt like that, but I definitely have."

"Hmm," mused Naomi, her eyes beginning to look back down.

"Just tell me," Gretchen said. "What the hell is going on? Why are you being so standoffish with me? Did I do something? Did I say something that offended you? I honestly don't know what's going on."

"Nothing," Naomi said with an obviously put-on smile. "You didn't do anything."

"Come on," said Gretchen. "You're being cagey. Did none of what happened… did that not affect you? I really thought we got *close*. You know?"

Naomi was beginning to look uncomfortable. She squirmed in her seat a bit and looked around, almost as though she were trying to make sure that nobody was listening in on their conversation. It took her a few more moments before she actually spoke up.

"I was just thinking," Naomi said quietly. "Maybe I'm *not*... you know.... like you."

"What?" Gretchen replied in an offended tone. "What do you mean?"

"Maybe I'm not gay," said Naomi with a shrug, her eyes looking down to her screen again.

"Hold on," said Gretchen. "That's insane. After everything you told me on the trip. After everything that *happened*."

"Can you keep your voice down?" said Naomi, looking around again. "I don't want the whole world to know our business."

"I'm just so flabbergasted," admitted Gretchen, putting her hand on her head. "How could you do such a one-eighty on this? I kind of feel like my heart's breaking." When she said this, Naomi's face grew a little more concerned and empathetic.

"It's just like..." Naomi said after another beat. "On the hike, we were out there in the wilderness. And that was Nova and Piggy. I just think that maybe, back here in real life, Naomi and Gretchen, maybe I should go back to how things were before."

"We *are* Nova and Piggy," Gretchen said firmly. "Your hiking name and personality, that's supposed to allow the *real* you out. It's not just some make believe game, Naomi. And I know for a fact that *was* the real you. I know it in my heart."

Naomi paused and took a deep breath, both of her hands bracing herself on the table as she absorbed what was happening. This conversation looked difficult for her. You could read it on her face. And although Gretchen knew Naomi's past and her struggles, it was hard for her to take all that into consideration when it felt like the girl she loved was snubbing her.

"I just *can't*," Naomi said, leaning in and whispering. "Gretchen, I can't. I'll lose my family. They'll disown me. You don't know what they're like."

"If they're so bad and close-minded," said Gretchen. "Maybe you should get away from them."

"It's just not that simple," protested Naomi. "They're my family, and I love them. And it's hard." When Naomi said this, her struggle became more real for Gretchen. She could see the pain on Naomi's face.

Gretchen sat back in her chair and folded her arms. She didn't know where to go from here or what to say. She loved Naomi, and she wanted to really start something with her best friend. Something meaningful and passionate and fun. But now Gretchen just felt lost.

"What about moving in together?" Gretchen asked solemnly. "What about you moving off of your parents' property and gaining some independence?"

"I don't know," Naomi replied. "I was thinking that maybe I'd stay a little longer, hopefully get this job, and start working on saving for a deposit for a house. It would probably only take me a year or two, max. I can tough it out at home a little longer."

"You are really twisting the knife," said Gretchen. "This is hurting me. My hopes got so high, and now you're just dashing them out. I feel like I might cry," she said, swiftly reaching up to blot her eye with a finger. "This is fucking crazy."

Naomi was looking upset as well, her expression communicating sorrow and confusion and worry. But she didn't say anything. It was like she was paralyzed.

"I love you, Naomi," said Gretchen. "And I know you're dealing with some heavy stuff. I'm here for you through all that. I can't promise it's going to be easy and pain-free. But I accept you for you. Okay? Just don't treat me like this. We went through so much together, so much struggle and pain hiking all that way and enduring the challenges and celebrating the successes. We're in this *together*. Don't push me away. I'm the one that's here for you."

"I know," Naomi said, averting her eyes.

Gretchen had gone from anger to acceptance quickly, and she was trying to be patient. But it was hard. She waited a little bit longer, to see if Naomi had anything else to say. Naomi, however, was silent and she wouldn't even look at Gretchen. After a moment, Gretchen sighed and she shut her laptop.

"I'll work on a letter for you and send it to HR at the credit union," Gretchen said. "Just get your application in. It looks like the new branches are opening in just a few months, so the sooner you can apply, the better."

"Okay," said Naomi solemnly.

"I think I'm going to take off," said Gretchen, removing

her laptop from the table and sliding it down into her bag. "If you want to talk, give me a call. Otherwise, I'll just see you at Dune City on our next shift together."

"I'm sorry, Gretchen."

"I am, too," she replied.

Gretchen stood up and she hefted her computer bag over her shoulder. Looking down at Naomi for a moment, she tried to search herself for the right words to say. But it was hard to be articulate and thoughtful when you felt so bad. Naomi flashed her eyes upward for one more glance at Gretchen and Gretchen just looked back at her with a sober face and flat lips.

"I'm sorry," Naomi said again.

"I'll talk to you soon, okay?" said Gretchen. "See you around."

Gretchen walked off, leaving Naomi sitting there alone in the cafe. Picking up her pace, Gretchen wanted to get outside before she began to cry, but the tears started just as she pushed the glass door open. She was devastated.

ALTHOUGH GRETCHEN KNEW that Naomi's actions could easily be explained by her difficulty in coming out to her family, it didn't make the feelings of rejection any easier to stomach. Everything had felt so magical in the 100 Mile Wilderness. She wasn't wrong in really sensing a new bond formed between her and Naomi. But now that they were back in civilization, back home, Naomi was getting cold feet.

This had been a lifetime of difficulty for her and one trip out into the woods wouldn't be enough to soothe her sorrows.

But at the same time, Gretchen had really *felt* it. There had been a change in Naomi, and being able to live as Nova —if even for a week—had given her the freedom to explore how she really felt. Gretchen knew deep down that Naomi loved her, and that she wanted to be with her, but she only needed to figure out how to make it happen back in their everyday life.

Gretchen was not willing to give up on her friend just yet.

The girls were scheduled to work together at the brewery and Gretchen knew that she wouldn't be able to avoid bringing things up. But she also knew that they would be in public, at their place of work, with regular patrons and their manager Jim around. Putting Naomi on the spot in this situation would not be a very kind or advisable thing to do. But Gretchen knew she had to say something. She had to push the issue without being so obvious about it.

Throughout their afternoon working together, Gretchen and Naomi were friendly and cordial with one another. Naomi sort of acted like the conversation at the cafe had never happened, and while that made Gretchen sting just a bit, she kept reminding herself that Naomi was going through some stuff, it was certainly hard, and the best thing she could do for her was to be understanding about it and not get angry. Naomi knew how she felt, and Gretchen was sure she knew how Naomi felt in return.

There was a lull in customers, as there often was around dinner time on a weekday. There were two couples off in a corner, playing tabletop shuffleboard in pairs and on one side of the bar there were two regulars, Steve and Benny, both in their sixties, beer bellies, and bearded. It was quiet enough, so Gretchen thought it might be a good opportunity to get away with being a bit cagey herself.

Gretchen removed her phone from her pocket and started to scroll through it.

"Ah ha," said Gretchen, putting on a smile. "There we go."

"What's up?" Naomi asked with interest. The two of them were hanging around the middle of the long bar, perched at the ready in case any new customers arrived.

"I've got a date," Gretchen said matter-of-factly.

"What? Who?"

"This girl Patti," said Gretchen. "I dated her off and on around the time I first arrived here in TC. But she ended up moving back to Detroit for a while. Now she's here again, she reached out, and we're going to see where it goes. You'd like her. She's super sweet."

Naomi was silent for a moment, almost pouting. But then she adjusted herself and stood up straight.

"That's nice," she said.

"Is it?"

"Yeah," said Naomi. "It's nice for you."

"Does it make you have any feelings?" Gretchen asked.

"I don't know," Naomi replied with a shrug.

"I don't have a date with Patti," confirmed Gretchen. "I just wanted to see your response."

"So you're screwing with me?" said Naomi in a huff. "That's pretty mean."

"The only person I want to go on a date with is you," Gretchen said candidly. "Full stop. But it seems like I can't have that. So I should probably move on, right? I should probably put you back in the mental compartment of 'friend' and find someone else to call girlfriend. Otherwise, there might be a lot of resentment between us."

"I don't want to talk about this here," Naomi replied, crossing her arms.

"It's quiet," said Gretchen. "We have six customers and they're all taken care of right now."

"I just mean at work," countered Naomi. "I don't want to talk about it at work."

"All right," Gretchen agreed. "Well, how about this? I went to the Timberline management office yesterday and talked to them about getting into a two-bedroom. They said they've got a waiting list for one-bedrooms like mine, so if I wanted to change it would be really easy to find someone else to take over my lease. We wouldn't have to wait for my lease to end to get an apartment together. It could happen next month."

Naomi looked side to side, checking to make sure the customers were all good and that nobody new was entering the tasting room. After a moment, she took Gretchen by the arm and led her through a swinging door into the back room where all the keg barrels were setup. The entire room was chilled to keep the beer at the appropriate temperature.

"I'm sorry, all right?" Naomi said with urgency. "This is really hard for me and my head feels like it's going to explode."

Gretchen immediately felt bad for the teasing she had just done. She regretted it.

"Coming out for me isn't going to be as easy as it was for you," Naomi continued. "And honestly, I don't know how to do this or what's going to happen."

"I'm sorry," Gretchen said, feeling guilty. She kept her eyes on Naomi.

"It's *different* here," said Naomi. "My family is conservative and religious, and even though I don't agree with that stuff I still love them and I still want them in my life."

"I know," Gretchen replied. "I'm really sorry, Naomi. I shouldn't have kept pushing."

"The hike," Naomi said, her passions still high. "That was like the best thing that has ever happened to me. Getting to be out there with you, mostly alone, and being able to be affectionate and open… Gretch, that was a dream come true. I just don't know how to make it happen back home. I'm not as confident as you, and I'm not as free. But *of course* I want to be with you. Damn it, of course I do."

"I'm sorry," Gretchen said once more.

"And I just keep thinking about what that guy Guru said on the trail," Naomi went on. "To thine own self be true… about not faking it or living a false life or whatever, and it just feels so out of reach. You know how much it sucks to be almost thirty and feel like you can't be yourself around your family? It's *painful*, it really is."

"I know," said Gretchen with empathy. "God, I feel like such a bitch for poking you. I should have been more understanding of your situation. I guess I was just excited for how things would be when we got back. Or how I perceived they would be. I thought everything was going to be great. Easy and great."

"That's how I want it to be, too," mused Naomi. She sat down on a keg and put her head in her hands.

"I do love you, Naomi," Gretchen said with emotive eyes. "I want to make this work with you. I want us to be together."

"I do, too," Naomi agreed. "I don't know how I'm going to make this work. I feel like if I tell my family *anything*, I'll immediately be kicked out and they'll stop talking to me. When I think about it, it's bad. I can really see it being bad."

"Why don't you come over tonight?" Gretchen offered. "Stay over. We can talk about it and try to figure out a plan of attack." She stopped herself and shook her head. "Those are the wrong words. What I mean to say is… we can figure out a way forward for you. Even if your worst fears come true, it's important to be yourself and live *your* life. Like Guru said. He wasn't living the life he wanted and it was killing him. The same thing is happening to you."

"I know it is," Naomi said. "I can't keep on living like this. I need to feel like I can be me."

"Come over tonight, okay?" implored Gretchen once

again. "You can be yourself in my apartment. You don't have anything to fear there."

Naomi nodded slowly, but she didn't say anything. It had been an emotional couple of weeks since they returned from Maine, and Gretchen could tell it had really taken its toll on Naomi. Looking out through the small window in the door to the keg room, Gretchen saw that a new set of customers had arrived.

"We have people," she said. "Are you ready to go back out there?"

Naomi stood up. After a pause, she shimmied up to Gretchen and she wrapped her arms around her waist. Then, leaning in, Naomi instigated a slow but eager kiss, a kiss which Gretchen immediately and happily returned. The girls stood there for a few moments more in the coldness of the keg room, kissing and holding to one another.

To Naomi, the kiss felt like a huge release, an immense weight off her shoulders. And Gretchen felt similar, but she also knew that it wasn't over yet. There was still a pretty steep elevation that the two of them would have to climb together.

"REMEMBER when we were standing there waiting for that guy Theo to arrive with our food resupply?" said Naomi. She was sitting crosslegged on Gretchen's couch, holding a bottle of beer in both of her hands. Gretchen sat across from her, on the other side of the coffee table, perched on a floor pillow. "We were tired and barely had any food left and it was like… is he *coming*?" Gretchen smiled and laughed.

"And that was only midway through the hike," Gretchen added. "It's hard to believe the hike was only six days. When we were in it, it felt like such a long time." Her eyes glazed over as she thought about it, and then Gretchen absently took a sip of beer.

"I loved those British people," Naomi continued in her reminiscing. "They were so funny and animated."

"We met a lot of great people on the hike," Gretchen agreed. "A lot of weirdos."

"You think some of them thought *we* were the weirdos?"

"Most definitely," said Gretchen. She grinned.

"We are weirdos," said Naomi. "Everybody is."

"All right, so…" Gretchen pivoted. "Back to the topic at hand."

"The topic at hand," Naomi repeated with a distant gaze.

"I think you should be brave," said Gretchen. "You were brave to come with me on the hike. You showed a lot of courage and you did something that very few people will ever do. I think you're a strong and confident woman. And it will feel so much better to be open about who you are. It will feel freeing to finally get to be yourself."

"But what if they hate me?" asked Naomi. "What if they stop speaking to me?"

"You can't control how other people think and feel," said Gretchen. "It sucks, but that's how it goes. Being a people pleaser, just going along and doing what other people want you to do, it damages the soul. It takes guts to live life on your own terms, and I think you'll find you get rewarded for being so valiant."

"I hope so," Naomi said, taking another drink. It had really sunk in for her how deep she was into all this. Her anger had subsided into acceptance. But now she just wanted to get to the other side.

"If your family really loves you, they will accept you," said Gretchen. "And it might take them some time to realize this. Real life stories don't always have happy endings, but if you matter to them more than bigotry and hatred, they'll come around."

"I don't think they're really bigoted or hateful people," Naomi proposed.

"Then that's good," said Gretchen. "But if they react adversely right away, just give them space. And you're allowed to be sad, too. You just have to realize that you're not at fault, you're not bad, and you're not wrong."

"I really liked when I was Nova," Naomi said, a new smile moving over her. "I felt so fearless and confident. I didn't worry what people thought of me when they met me. I didn't really have *any* worries out there on the trail, to be honest. And after a long day of hiking, all I could really think about was crashing hard and getting some sleep."

"That's who you *are*," Gretchen implored. "You are Nova. You just need to figure out how to bridge the gap between being on the trail and living your normal life. I know you can do it. Just summon that same strength we had to find when we knew we just had a few more miles until a campsite. You just keep pushing."

"Yeah," Naomi said, letting Gretchen's words marinate. "I know you're right. I feel this confidence and strength inside of me. It's just a little dormant. It's just under the surface."

"It's bubbling up," Gretchen said matter-of-factly. "I can feel it."

Naomi smiled. She could feel it, too.

The night carried on, and the girls gleefully remembered their trip. It had only been two weeks but it was beginning to feel so distant. They had both recovered already. Their knees, their calves, their ankles, their feet, it all felt back to normal. With the aches and pains subsiding, it made the hike feel all that much more in the past. But it was nice to talk about it, to gloat to one another about what a big thing they had done. And it was exciting to talk about other similar trips that they might want to make in the future.

"Are you going to stay over?" Gretchen asked tenderly. The girls both stood near the kitchen after cleaning up, holding each other's hands, feeling a small buzz from the beers they had drank.

"I don't know," said Naomi coyly. She smiled. "Why should I?"

"Because I love you," Gretchen said, leaning in and kissing her. "And I love being with you."

"Mmm," Naomi hummed in response. She now kissed Gretchen. "I love you, too. You're my best friend, and you're the only person I want to be with."

"So stay," said Gretchen.

"Okay," Naomi agreed easily, planting another kiss on Gretchen's lips. "I'll stay."

It didn't take that much more back and forth before the girls ended up in Gretchen's bed together. They laughed and kissed and explored each other joyfully, the first time they had gone to bed since returning from their adventure. It was something they had both missed, being next to each other in the dark of the night. And this time it was all the more comfortable, not having to sleep on the ground or in a hammock, or even in that small single bed at the Hiker Hostel. Gretchen's bed was much bigger and softer than any of that.

Naomi gave herself over to the passion, and it felt so freeing to spread her legs wide and have Gretchen dive in. It was exactly the kind of thing she imagined when she imagined having sex. She had imagined it with her first crush Lily so long ago, she had imagined it with a few other women since then, and she imagined it with Gretchen ever since the two had met. To have Gretchen's tongue exploring her soft, wet flesh, sending shivers of desire throughout her limbs, it gave Naomi goosebumps and it made her feel like her heart was going to rip out of her chest.

At one point, they ended up in a sixty-nine, and she felt the excitement overtake her as Gretchen pleasured her below all while Naomi stared up into her lover's pussy, using her thumb to caress it back and forth through its wetness. Gretchen slowly lowered herself, and as her middle closed in on Naomi's face, Naomi eagerly opened her mouth and began to eat Gretchen out. It felt wonderful—for both of them—but particularly for Naomi, who was walking on air as she felt how spectacular it was to both give and receive at the same time.

It all felt so natural, and so right. With Gretchen, Naomi didn't feel like she was a square peg trying to fit into a round hole. In fact, when she was with Gretchen, all holes felt appropriate and fitting for Naomi. Perched on her knees on the floor at the foot of the bed, Naomi eagerly licked and sucked at Gretchen's pussy, with Gretchen's legs spread and draped wide off of the bed. With her lips focused on Gretchen's clit, Naomi pushed two fingers inside of her and began slowly and methodically penetrating her. The noises coming from Gretchen and her writhing on the bed gave Naomi all the confidence she needed to continue.

And when Gretchen finally burst in a series of moans and convulsions, Naomi felt indescribably pleased. Her sense of accomplishment filled her with both gratitude and faith. Faith that this was right, that this was where she was supposed to be. But most of all, watching Gretchen climax filled Naomi with a deeper sense of love for her best friend. It made her want to do it again and again. It made her want Gretchen to be happy like that forever.

The girls laid next to each other in bed, sweaty and happy, Gretchen with an arm around Naomi and cuddling up together. Gretchen played with a few strands of Naomi's dark hair, adoring and loving her, while Naomi's sense of accomplishment continued to thrive. There was no other place she wanted to be and for once in her life was finally beginning to feel like it was on track. And it was all thanks to Gretchen. Gretchen, whether she meant to or not, had been the driving force for Naomi to come out of her shell. And life outside that container felt fantastic.

"Thank you," cooed Naomi happily, she leaned her face over and kissed Gretchen on the shoulder.

"For what?" Gretchen replied, her face beaming in post-orgasmic bliss.

"For everything," confirmed Naomi. "Thanks for being there for me, thanks for pushing me even when I didn't want to be pushed. Thanks for loving me for who I am."

"I'll always be here for you," said Gretchen. "I love you so much."

"I love you, too."

Naomi rolled over and pushed against Gretchen now, and they resumed kissing and fondling and hugging. The night was still young, and there was more love to explore. And Naomi, finally starting to find herself and see herself for who she truly was, couldn't get enough. Desire was in her bones, and she wanted to be there in bed with Gretchen for all eternity.

A FEW DAYS LATER, Gretchen and Naomi went together to the front office of the Timberline apartment complex. There was an open two-bedroom available and they immediately put down a deposit to hold it while they got everything lined up. Naomi still hadn't told her family that she was planning to move out of the backyard cottage—and nor had she told them her much more important news—but she was thrilled nonetheless that the wheels were in motion to move in with Gretchen. Every moment she spent with Gretchen, now that she was finally beginning to accept her own feelings, was filled with happiness and excitement.

They traded off whose place they slept at, but they stayed with one another most nights. It reminded them, in a way, of how it had been when they were on their hike. It just felt right to sleep side by side, and any night spent alone felt disappointing and lacking. After one particular evening spent over at Naomi's, the girls woke up early, lazily drank a few cups of coffee together, and got to work packing up Naomi's things and preparing to move her life over to the new apartment.

"Should we hide the boxes?" Gretchen asked, setting a big box, open and full of clothes, down on the couch. "I mean, if they look in the windows, they'll know something is up."

"They don't ever come down here," said Naomi. "I'm not worried."

"I'm a little worried that you haven't told them yet, to be honest," Gretchen warned. "You're going to hit them with this and it's going to seem like you've been sneaking around and keeping things from them."

"Well..." Naomi said. "I guess I *have*." She smiled and shrugged.

"But I thought your thing was that you don't want to damage your relationship," Gretchen pushed. "Don't you think you'll do exactly that if you tell them you're moving out and do it the next day?"

"Yeah, maybe," Naomi reluctantly agreed. She dropped the box she'd been holding down onto a table and paused to think about Gretchen's words. "I guess I just don't know yet how to put it all out there."

"I can be there if you want," offered Gretchen.

"I don't know if that would be a good idea," replied Naomi. "I just don't know how it's all going to go down."

"You should do it soon," said Gretchen. "At least tell them you're moving. I know coming out can be much harder, and you should wait until you're really ready for that."

"I'll go tell them now," Naomi said with resolve after another moment of thought. "Why not? I should just do it. Pull the bandage off."

"That you're moving or that you're gay… or both?" asked Gretchen.

"I don't know," Naomi said. "My Dad isn't even home right now. He should be at work. Though my Mom is."

"So you're going to go tell your Mom right now?"

"Yes," Naomi said. A smile moved over her face.

"Do you want me to come with you?"

"No, it's fine," said Naomi. "I'll be right back."

And with those simple words, Naomi moved to the door of her little cottage and she walked through it. Gretchen watched her with a bit of confusion, the puzzlement written on her face. But at the same time, she was proud that Naomi was taking the reins. The confident Nova was starting to make herself known.

Naomi walked through the yard and up to her parents' home. It was only past nine in the morning, and there was a crisp breeze outside. She moved with authority and courage, feeling as though she could do this. There was nothing to be afraid of. She was, after all, a grown woman and she could do whatever she wanted.

Entering through the side door and moving into the kitchen, Naomi almost immediately saw her mother, who was sitting at the kitchen counter and working out a grocery list on a small notepad.

"Hey," Naomi said, stopping in her tracks as she felt a wave of nervousness wash over her. She pushed through it, though, and she put on a brave face.

"Hello, dear," said her mother with a half-smile. "Good morning."

"Morning," Naomi replied. She took a few steps closer to where her mother sat. "Can I talk to you for a moment?"

"Yes, of course," her mother replied. She put her pen down. "What's going on?"

"A lot's been going on," admitted Naomi. "I applied for a job at a credit union, and I already heard back. They want to set up a phone interview next week, and if that works out I'll have to drive down to Lansing for an in-person."

"You're not planning to move to Lansing, are you?" her mother asked with uncertainty.

"No," said Naomi. "They're opening a branch here."

"Oh," her mother mused. She smiled. "That's great, I'm

really happy for you. I've been hoping that you'd move on from your bar job and get something a little more stable."

"I'm happy about it, too," Naomi said with a smile. "I'm excited to see what happens. I also have other news."

"Other news," her mother repeated. "What's that?"

"I'm moving out," Naomi conferred with a new light in her eyes. "I'm signing a lease on an apartment with my friend Gretchen."

"Well, all right!" her mother said with a short laugh. "I might think you'd wait until you actually *got* this new job before committing to signing a lease, but it is probably time for you to move out on your own. I'm glad you found a friend that you would be happy to live with."

"Thanks," Naomi said. She paused. It had been so much easier than she had built up in her mind, and because of this ease her confidence was soaring. Naomi felt good about herself and about her new direction. "I've got another thing. Another thing to tell you."

"Well, you sure have a lot going on," her mother said. "All right. What else have you got?"

"My friend Gretchen," Naomi began. "That I'm moving in with. She's not just my friend. Mom, she's my girlfriend." Her mother looked confused.

"Your friend Gretchen that you went to Maine to hike with," said her mother. "She's your… girlfriend? I'm not sure I understand, dear."

"I think you do…" Naomi said slowly.

"I…" her mother replied, still seeming like she wasn't able to put it together. "I'm not sure."

"I'm gay, Mom," Naomi said, her eyes beginning to water a bit but she held tightly to her confidence. "I've felt it for a very long time, but I haven't been able to admit it to myself. Well, here I am admitting it now. I know it might be hard or shocking, but I'm still your daughter and I still love this family and I hope nothing changes between us. I just wanted you to know, okay?"

Her mother crossed her arms. She didn't look angry, just perplexed. It was almost as though Naomi's words weren't fully sinking in.

"Don't tell Dad yet," Naomi went on. "I want to tell him myself. And please don't hate me or think I'm wrong or bad or going to hell. I'm not any of those things. I'm just me and I'm just trying to be happy and be myself. I need to make these changes to really start to find myself. I hope you understand."

"Honey… you're *gay*?" asked her mother skeptically.

"Yes," said Naomi. "I am."

"I just… all right," said her mother. There was a look of sadness and confusion moving over her, and it made Naomi feel sad and confused as well.

"I'm gonna go," said Naomi. "I'm packing some things right now, getting ready for the move. I'm not sure exactly when we're going to move, but probably in the next week or two. I'll let you know."

"Thank you, dear."

"All right," Naomi said, feeling the weird tension in the room. "I'm going." She offered a consolation smile, and her mother half-smiled in kind. With a small wave, Naomi turned from where she stood in her parents' kitchen and she exited the same way she entered. She felt better that it was out in the open, but she still didn't feel good.

Naomi took her time walking back down to her cottage in the backyard. She had ripped the bandage off, and she was still feeling the sting of it. When she had played it through in her mind, she imagined her mother getting angry when she told her that she was gay, or getting defensive or confrontational. But she was just disappointed. She acquiesced. It made Naomi feel disheartened, when all she really wanted to feel was acceptance.

When she opened the door to the cottage, waiting for her on the other side with a big expectant smile was Gretchen. Gretchen lit up the room, and she lit up Naomi's life. The discouragement she had just been feeling evaporated when she saw her girlfriend, and Naomi's smile grew to match Gretchen's.

"Well?" Gretchen asked. "How did it all go?"

When Naomi unloaded all of her news to her father later on, his response was similar to how her mother had reacted. It was mostly just tight-lipped disappointment, and it hurt Naomi to sense this. But it was far better than her worst case scenario. Both of her parents were positive about her going for a better job and moving out on her own. Surprisingly, her mother had been a little more upbeat about Naomi coming out, even going as far as to say that it was important for Naomi to be herself, but it was still obvious that their religious beliefs were causing them confusion in how to process their daughter's truth.

Still, Naomi felt much better. It was like the weight of the world had been lifted from her. And suddenly it began to make sense to her why she had been living in such a state of arrested development. It had been impossible to launch her life when she was hiding such a secret, and it stunted her growth as an adult. But now, with her sexuality out in the open—at least with her family—and Gretchen by her side, life was taking on a new color for Naomi. The future looked promising.

In what felt like a throwback to their big hike, the girls sat together on the top step of the staircase that lead to their new joint apartment. They had spent the morning moving Naomi's things from the cottage at her parents' place, and were now taking a break for water and snacks. Each had their own wide-mouthed water bottle and a small bag of trail mix. Although it was now September, it was still quite warm in Traverse City and they were dressed similar in short polyester running shorts, tank tops, and sneakers. They both wore their hair up, and Gretchen had a cap on. Naomi's cheeks were pink and she tilted her head back to take a big gulp of water.

"It's hotter than I thought it would be today," she mused.

"Yeah, it's really warmed up this morning," agreed Gretchen. "It might be a rough afternoon moving my stuff over from the other building, seeing as I've got the bulk of the furniture."

"Is your bed heavy?"

"It's not bad," said Gretchen. "It's memory foam, and there's no box spring. So it's not as heavy as a normal bed."

"How are you feeling?" Naomi asked. "Okay?"

"I'm okay," said Gretchen. "It is tougher than I thought carrying this stuff up two flights of stairs in the heat. When I moved, it was colder out."

"I feel like it wasn't even this warm in Maine," said Naomi, now laying her head on Gretchen's shoulder.

"Well, we were kind of up in the mountains there," Gretchen replied with a laugh. She then turned her face and kissed Naomi on the head.

"That's true."

"But don't worry," continued Gretchen. "This will be all over before you know it. And we'll order a pizza and have a cold beer and relax in our new apartment together." She smiled big, and as her words set in, Naomi also grew a big smile.

"That's right," Naomi said. "I'm so happy about it."

"I am, too," said Gretchen. "It's amazing."

"Some days I feel like I'm dreaming," Naomi conferred. "These past few weeks—ever since we returned from the hike, actually—I can't tell if I'm living in reality or if I'm in a dream. Pinch me."

"Okay," Gretchen said, reaching over to Naomi's side and moving in to follow her command.

"No, no!" Naomi countered, already laughing. "Don't pinch me."

Gretchen did anyway, pinching Naomi's side and making a big production of it. Naomi squealed and batted her hand away.

"I'm too ticklish!" Naomi burst out.

"Then you shouldn't have said anything," Gretchen warned with a wry grin.

"Just kiss me, okay?" said Naomi.

"I can do that," Gretchen said. Leaning in, she pressed her lips to Naomi's and they sat there on the step for a few tender moments, kissing one another with joy in their hearts.

Things were moving fast, but Naomi felt like she was making up for lost time. When you feel like things are going your way and you're living your dream, it's easy to be impatient because you want it all. And Naomi was certainly eager to have it all. Her phone interview with the credit union had been great, and they invited her down to Lansing to meet in person. In addition, Gretchen had called up her old boss Jodie and put in a glowing recommendation for her girlfriend. It actually felt good to talk to Jodie, and it reminded Gretchen of the good times she had at the job rather than some of the more tedious. Jodie also put a bug in Gretchen's ear.

"I know you're off doing your own thing," Jodie had said. "And I respect that, even though we do miss you around here. I mentioned to Dale that I had heard from you and he looked like a lightbulb went off over his head."

"Yeah?" Gretchen replied with interest.

"Dale was recently promoted to management in mortgage lending," Jodie continued. "And he wondered if maybe you would be looking for a job up there in Traverse City. He thought you'd enjoy the position and had enough knowledge to transition into the mortgage department."

"Dale said that?" said Gretchen in astonishment.

"He did," Jodie confirmed. "So if it's something you would be interested in, you should reach out to him. I know they're hiring now for when the branches open up there."

"Okay," Gretchen agreed cautiously. "Thanks Jodie."

"No problem," said Jodie. "And thank you for the recommendation for Naomi. I think she'd be a good fit."

Gretchen hadn't told Naomi any of this, as it had only recently happened before their move. But in their break in lugging stuff up the stairs, sitting their on the step trying to catch their breath and reenergize, the thought came to Gretchen that she should share what Jodie had told her.

"That's awesome, Gretch," Naomi beamed. "There could be some real money in that. I mean, getting into mortgage lending, you probably get commissions and such. Right?"

"Yeah, maybe," said Gretchen. "I just don't know, though. I really love my freedom of working part-time and being able to go off and do what I please. I don't know if I would have been able to hike the 100 Mile Wilderness if I had a full-time job again."

"And yet you're pushing me toward a full-time job," Naomi teased, bumping her shoulder into Gretchen's with a laugh.

"I just knew you were looking for a change," said Gretchen. "And it could be really awesome for you."

"I'm just playing around," Naomi said and smiled. "But you should reach out to your old coworker and see what his offer is. Who knows? You might even be able to make your own hours and still keep that freedom you love so much."

"I don't know," said Gretchen. "I'm not sure what the job would be."

"Then *call* him," Naomi pushed. "Why not? If it's not your thing, you don't have to do it."

"Yeah," Gretchen replied. A smile crept over her face. "Okay, I'll call Dale and see what he says. It has been over a year and a half since I worked at the credit union. I feel like I've got some of the angst out of my system."

"And then we could work together," Naomi offered, playing the tape forward. "We could go out to lunch together, take a stroll down Front Street, laugh and smile and just generally be awesome together. It sounds pretty good to me!" Gretchen laughed and shook her head.

"You're hilarious," she said. "And I love you for it." They kissed.

"I love you, too," Naomi responded, a blissful look plastered on her face.

"Do you think we should get back to work?"

"Ugh," groaned Naomi. "Yeah, probably. I'm still sweating my ass off, though." She lifted her arm up and used her tank top to wipe the sweat from under her armpit.

"You hiked a hundred miles in the remote wilderness," Gretchen said in mock-seriousness. "You climbed thousands of feet in elevation. I think you can hike some furniture up a few steps."

"I know," Naomi said, grinning. She kissed her lover once more and then she quickly jumped up from where she sat. "So what are we doing now?"

"We're taking the moving truck across the complex to my old spot, we're loading it up, and then we're bringing it all over here," Gretchen said, she herself now standing.

"I'm ready," Naomi said. "Hold on." She poured the rest of her water into her mouth and then sighed in refreshment.

Stepping up onto the landing, Naomi walked into their new apartment and approached the sink to refill her water bottle. She looked around the mostly empty apartment, some of her own boxes piled up in the living room, a few of them sitting on the kitchen counter, and she smiled wide to herself. This felt like such an incredible new beginning for Naomi, and it made her feel just as she felt when she had hiked up those high mountains in Maine. It was a similar feeling of accomplishment. And to Naomi, accomplishment wasn't something she was used to feeling. It felt great on her.

Turning from the sink, she caught Gretchen watching her with a happy smile on her face from the open door. Naomi, still smiling herself, recapped her water bottle with a plucky spin and sashayed over to her best friend in the world.

"Okay," she said. "*Now* I'm ready."

Gretchen sat out on the porch, overlooking a pond with a fountain spouting out a cascade of water. She was home alone for now, as Naomi had made a run to her parents' house to take care of a few things, though she would be back soon as they both had work at Dune City in just about an hour. Gretchen looked down into her phone for a few moments as she contemplated what she was about to do. She thought back to the hike and she meditated on how it changed her. Compromise and balance were important, something she had difficulty with in the past. But now, her life was starting to feel like it was taking shape. Being with Naomi felt like a missing piece of a puzzle.

After quenching her thirst with a glass of iced tea, she navigated through her contact list and quickly found the name she was looking for. Gretchen hit the call button and she raised the phone to her ear. She waited as it rung.

"Midwest Michigan Federal Credit Union," said the voice. "This is Dale Vernier, how can I help you?"

"Dale," said Gretchen. "It's Gretchen Slate. How are you?"

"Whoa, Gretchen Slate," Dale replied. "How in the heck are you?"

"I'm good," Gretchen said with a smile. "Really good. I was talking with Jodie recently and she said you might want to talk to me."

"Right!" said Dale. "You were connecting your girlfriend to Jodie for a potential job up at our new branch in Traverse City."

"That's right," Gretchen said. "And she told me you were promoted."

"Yeah, I'm a manager now in the mortgage lending department," said Dale. "It's awesome. I moved out of the branch office and I'm now at the main office. I'm loving it."

"Congratulations," Gretchen offered. "That's great, Dale. I'm really happy for you."

"And they put me in charge of starting the lending program up there in TC," he said. "We're getting so close to the grand opening, it's really sneaking up on us."

"When should the branches open?"

"A month maybe," said Dale. "Definitely by the end of October. We're just waiting on the construction crew to complete the build outs. We'll have one location down on Front Street, and another a bit further out in Garfield Township. I'll have both branches staffed with loan officers. And that's why I mentioned to Jodie that I might like to talk to you."

"All right," said Gretchen. "Let's talk."

"You're obviously really good at client facing work," said Dale. "You were always a friendly and helpful teller and our members liked you. Everybody in the branch liked you."

"That's nice of you to say."

"Being a loan officer is similar," he went on. "You're working a bit more intimately with our members, but you're helping them through some complex things and helping them with—let's face it—the biggest purchase of their life. It's always good to have a friendly face in that role, someone they feel like they can trust and feel comfortable around. I think that's you."

"You know, I really don't have much experience in mortgages," Gretchen countered. "I haven't even bought my own house yet."

"Don't worry about that," said Dale. "We'll train you. It's more about the personality, and you've got that. We know you're trustworthy and reliable, because you've already worked with the credit union for a number of years. I just want to put it out there that I think you'd be great in the position and we'd love to have you back."

"One of the reasons I left, Dale," Gretchen admitted. "Was that I was looking for a change, looking for more time to myself, more freedom. I recently did a huge hike out in Maine. A hundred miles in the wilderness over six days. That's not an every day kind of thing, obviously, but I'd really like the freedom to take longer stretches like that off to go on big trips and have those experiences. You know what I mean?"

"Absolutely," said Dale. "I think we'll be able to work it with HR so that if you came back, you'd get to keep the seniority and your allowed PTO from your previous time working with us. So you would have a decent amount of vacation days. Plus, being a loan officer, you are a step up in the organization and eventually—relatively soon, actually—you would probably have four weeks of time off for PTO. That's pretty good, right?"

"Yeah, it's good," Gretchen agreed.

"Obviously, I'm not going to beg," said Dale. "You

should do what you're going to do. But I knew you moved up to Traverse City, and we always got along, and I know you were a good employee of the credit union. So if you want to come back and work for me, I can make it happen easily. You won't even need to apply. I can email you the offer and as soon as you sign it, we'll reactivate you and you're back. That's it."

"Wow," Gretchen said, carefully thinking about it. As much as she had loved her time working slower, less professional jobs, Dale's offer was enticing. Now that things were going well with Naomi, that they had got a place together and were really getting closer, it felt like it made sense to start building a life together. And Gretchen had turned thirty. Part-time, lifestyle jobs wouldn't cut it forever. It was a tough decision, and she would definitely have to think harder about it.

"Tell you what," said Dale. "I'll send you our offer tomorrow, with whatever addendums need to be made for your seniority within the company, and you can think it over. You can call me with any questions or concerns. We've got a little time on this, but like I said… we're looking at opening in just about a month, and I really need to get a few more people in as loan officers so we can start expanding up north. That sound good?"

"Yeah, Dale," said Gretchen. "That does sound good. Thanks for thinking of me. I'm going to think about it and I'll let you know very soon, within a couple of days of receiving the offer. I promise I won't leave you hanging."

"Excellent," said Dale. "I'm really looking forward to

working with you again, Gretch. *And* maybe I can get you into a house of your own soon enough." Gretchen laughed.

"We'll see," she said. "Thanks again. I'll talk to you soon, Dale."

"Take it easy, Gretchen," he said. "Have a great day."

Gretchen hung up her cell phone and placed it down onto the small patio table in front of her. She smiled gently and stared out into the pond, absently watching the water feature do its thing amid a cool breeze wafting in to her apartment balcony. Everything felt so idyllic and easy. Maybe she had found what she was looking for, and the universe was giving her a second chance to embrace her old career in a new way. She had run away to find herself, and it really felt like the risk was paying off.

She heard the apartment door unlock inside and she turned her head to look through the screen door from the balcony. In walked Naomi, dressed casually in summer clothes to beat the heat, carrying a single box under her arm. Naomi caught Gretchen looking and she waved, prompting Gretchen to smile and wave back. Shutting the door behind her, Naomi tossed her car keys onto the counter and set her box down. She then sauntered over to the screen door, opened it, and stepped outside on the porch.

"Hello," said Naomi. Leaning down, she kissed Gretchen sweetly.

"Hi there," Gretchen said. "How was it?"

"Eh," Naomi replied, rolling her hand back and forth. "I think it's dawning on them and they're beginning to accept it. It just feels weird. But I guess it's felt weird over there for a long time."

"That's okay," Gretchen consoled. "The upside is that your worst fears didn't come true. They didn't disown you."

"That's true," Naomi agreed. "I'm hoping that they just need some time, and things will get back to normal soon."

"I hope so, too," Gretchen said with a warm smile.

"I searched all over in that house," said Naomi. "I really thought I had something I could wear to the interview. Some kind of suit. But I just don't."

"That's okay," said Gretchen. "I told you you could borrow something of mine. I have professional clothes."

"I'll do that," Naomi agreed. She kissed Gretchen once more. "Mmm."

"I just got off the phone with my old coworker, Dale," said Gretchen. "He offered me a job as a loan officer at one of the new branches up here."

"He did!" beamed Naomi. "Gretchen, that's amazing. Are you going to take it?"

"I think so," said Gretchen. "I want to think about it a little bit more, but it's a good opportunity. And hey, we could carpool." Naomi laughed.

"Well, I don't *quite* have an offer yet," she said. "But if I do get the job, and you *take* the job, then yes… we can carpool."

"But for now," Gretchen concluded. "We should get ready and then head over to Dune City."

"Are you going to put in your notice today?"

"Not yet," said Gretchen. "Not until I really make the decision."

"Okay," Naomi said, smiling happily and excitedly. She reached down and took Gretchen's hand, helping her up out of her seat. As she came to her feet, Gretchen wrapped her arms around Naomi and the two fell into a deep embrace together.

The love was palpable.

IT WAS late in the afternoon about a week or so later, and Gretchen stood behind the bar at Dune City with Jim by her side. They had a handful of customers sitting at the bar, a few more groups at the table, and some more people sitting outside on the patio. Even though tourist season in Traverse City had come and gone, they were still quite busy for late September. The weather was nice and the locals felt more at ease, and that translated to people coming out on that later afternoon, the last Friday before October.

With everybody having their beer for the moment, Gretchen and Jim were cleaning up and preparing for the next rounds. Gretchen washed the pint glasses, while Jim did the necessary maintenance on the taps, wiping them down and making sure they poured clean. Gretchen had a lot on her mind, but it was all good. She felt content, ready to take on whatever came next, and for the first time in a while, not feeling the insatiable wanderlust that had defined the last couple of years for her.

"It should die down in about an hour," mused Jim, stepping up next to Gretchen and leaning on the bar.

"Yep," agreed Gretchen. "Dinner time is closing in."

"This might be the last big Friday for a while," said Jim. "I think we're going to have to start cutting hours."

"That's all right," Gretchen replied. She stood back from the washing station and wiped her hands on a white towel. "Actually, about that..."

"Yeah?"

Gretchen had already quit the knife store, but she wanted to stay on at Dune City to see the summer season out. She also didn't want to spring it all at once on Jim, the possibility of both her and Naomi leaving. Naomi's fate was still uncertain, but Gretchen had made her decision. The credit union was opening in just a matter of weeks, and she had made her commitment to Dale. Gretchen was returning to full-time work.

"I accepted another job," Gretchen admitted. "It's at the credit union I used to work at down in Lansing. They're opening up here and, well, I took a job with them."

"Oh, that's great," said Jim with a smile. "That's awesome, Gretchen. I mean, you know hours here go down the tubes in winter. And I'm sure it's a better job than this, anyway. More money and stability and all that."

"Right," said Gretchen. "I just felt like it was time. I should have enough vacation to do my adventuring, and besides... there's so much nature and hiking to explore here in Traverse City, it'll take me forever to exhaust what we have up here."

"That's right," Jim confirmed. "Tons up here. And plus you could easily head to the U.P. and explore up there. Lots of camping and hiking."

"Thanks for understanding," Gretchen replied, smiling happily. "I'm excited for the next step and to see where this all takes me. I'm really loving it up here and I feel like I'm finally finding my place. Only took a year and a half."

"So when do you start the new job?" asked Jim.

"End of October, probably," she said. "But by the middle of October I have to be available for some training."

"You're leaving that soon, eh?" Jim remarked. "Well, all right. That's how it goes, I guess. Hopefully some of the others are planning on sticking around so I don't have to do any new hiring."

"Yeah," Gretchen said absently. She still wasn't sure about Naomi's status, but she knew they would find out soon enough.

It closed in on half past six and the customers began filtering out. It was nice and predictable that they would leave for dinner, and there would be about an hour break before different customers wandered in for their Friday night drinks. Gretchen looked at her phone, eyeing the time, wondering when Naomi would make her entrance. But when she looked up once again, gazing out of the windows and into the parking lot, Gretchen saw Naomi's car pull into a spot and she got a big smile.

Naomi came waltzing in with a happy and bright face, wearing a dark grey wool blazer with matching pants, a white blouse, and black heels. Her dark hair was brushed and smooth, falling straight down and framing her made-up visage. Gretchen was excited to see her, and she rushed around from the back of the bar, closed in on Naomi, and gave her a big hug.

"How did it go?" Gretchen asked, kissing Naomi's ear after she spoke.

"Great," Naomi replied. "Just great."

"Let's have a beer!" Gretchen suggested, and Naomi nodded enthusiastically.

As the girls approached the bar—Gretchen behind it, Naomi sitting on a stool at it—Jim got a curious and questioning look on his face as he spotted Naomi. It was very strange to see her so dressed up.

"What's all this?" Jim asked, motioning with a single finger at Naomi's attire.

"I went down to Lansing today for an interview," Naomi said blithely.

"Whoa, really?" replied Jim. "That's a lot of driving for one day."

"Three hours each way," Naomi said. She accepted a beer from Gretchen happily and took an eager sip from the small glass.

"Okay, so what's going on here?" Jim asked, looking back and forth between the girls. "Are you *both* leaving me?"

"I'm sorry, Jim," Gretchen said empathetically.

"So, you too?" Jim said, looking now to Naomi.

"Yeah," Naomi confirmed. "I got a new job."

"In *Lansing*?" said Jim.

"No, it's up here," said Naomi. "The interview was down there."

"And when do you start?"

"Late October," Naomi said.

"That's the same as Gretchen," Jim replied, lifting an eyebrow.

"We're going to be working at the same place," Gretchen said with a smile. "We can't get away from each other."

"I guess not," Jim said with a hint of exasperation. "Okay, well now I really have to make sure we're covered for the coming months."

"I'm sorry," said Naomi. "This is my first real job. I'm pretty excited about it."

"No, no," Jim said, putting his palms up. "Don't be sorry. I understand. This is what you've got to do. Both of you. I completely understand."

"Thanks, Jim," Gretchen said, reaching over and squeezing his shoulder.

"We'll be fine," he replied. "Really, we will. I just hope you two won't be strangers."

"We live right across the street," said Naomi with a laugh. "I think we'll be back." Gretchen smiled and nodded in agreement.

"I think I'm going to have to fix next month's schedule," Jim thought out loud. "If you two are both gone…" he mused and held up a finger. "Be right back."

Jim then scurried off from behind the bar and made his way to the back room.

"So you got it?" Gretchen said, eyes bright as she grinned across the bar at Naomi.

"I got it," Naomi confirmed happily. "I can't believe it. They offered me the job right there and it's a done deal. I'm going to get trained and then I'll be sitting there at the counter on day one. It's craziness to me, but I'm so excited and ready for this new chapter in my life. I feel great, Gretch. I feel just amazing."

"You *are* amazing," Gretchen said. "And I'm so proud of you."

"Oh, there's one more thing," Naomi said with a mischievous look in her eye.

"Yeah?" Gretchen questioned, noticing something was up.

"I told them I already had a trip planned," said Naomi. "In December. Plane tickets bought, all that."

"But we didn't plan anything yet," said Gretchen. Naomi just smiled big and shrugged.

"We will," she said. "It's my birthday, after all, and I'm turning thirty. I want to do something special… with you."

"I'll let Dale know that I've got those very same days already booked," Gretchen said, easily picking up her lover's mischievousness. "I'm guessing some sort of outdoor adventure?"

"I've got an idea," Naomi revealed. "I'll tell you about it later."

"*Later*?" said Gretchen impatiently. Naomi laughed and then took a gulp of her beer.

"Yeah," Naomi said. "I'm still figuring it out." Gretchen grinned and shook her head.

"All right," she said. "But you know this is going to eat me up. Don't keep me in suspense for too long."

"I'll have another beer, bar maid," Naomi teased, sliding her now empty glass back toward Gretchen. "You give me a half-pint, and I'm going to drink it quick."

"Yes, ma'am," Gretchen replied. She swiped the glass away and quickly washed it out. Then, turning to the row of taps she immediately went for the style she knew to be Naomi's favorite, a honey basil ale.

Naomi's eyes grew big as her new beer approached. It had been a long day. All that driving, and the stress of her first professional interview. She had earned it.

"Here you are," Gretchen said. As she placed the glass in front of Naomi, she leaned over the bar and kissed Naomi sweetly. Naomi hummed happily to herself, feeling love from all around her. It was nice to feel cared for, accepted, and appreciated.

As Naomi gulped from her second glass, drinking her favorite beer, Gretchen just watched with her arms crossed and a big smile. What more could she ask for?

WITH THE SUMMER coming to an end and school starting back up, the pool at the Timberline apartment complex was much less busy than it had been during the hottest months. Although with temperatures still pushing upwards of eighty degrees and the sun still high in the sky, Gretchen and Naomi decided to lay out and relax poolside in some of their final days before their work lives were to shift. The pool area next to the clubhouse was mostly empty on that early October day as the clock neared noon, and the girls both chilled into their sunning chairs in their bikinis and sunglasses. It felt good to take it easy.

There was still a lot to do. It would soon be Gretchen's turn to drive down to Lansing to meet with Dale and some other colleagues for training, while Naomi's training as a teller would be happening at the new branch before the doors officially opened. They each also had a couple more shifts at Dune City to fulfill, but this particular time at the beginning of October felt as though it fully belonged to them. They knew that soon enough they'd be dressing professional and heading to the credit union, but for now they could strip down, hit the pool, and enjoy life.

Gretchen lifted her water bottle to her mouth and took a drink, looking out over the pool in front of her through the shade of her sunglasses. She smiled happily to herself, the sun warming her, and a cool breeze from the bay making itself known every so often to temper the heat. Looking to her left, she watched adoringly as Naomi applied sunscreen to her stomach, rubbing the creamy lotion from one side to the other.

After a moment, Naomi looked up and caught Gretchen watching. She smiled and pursed her lips into a kiss.

"This could be one of the last really nice days of the season," said Gretchen.

"Yep," Naomi agreed, returning to applying her sunblock.

"At the beginning of summer," said Gretchen. "I never would have imagined things would end up as they have."

"Yeah, me either," Naomi said with a laugh.

"I couldn't fathom going back to full-time work," said Gretchen. "But neither did I have any clue you and I would end up together. It's amazing how quickly things can change. If you blink you might miss it. I feel like I did blink and when I opened my eyes again, my life got immensely better."

"Me too," said Naomi happily. She put her sunscreen down on a table and went for her water bottle. "For me, the catalyst was the hike. I mean, *no doubt.* Doing that changed me at my core. I'd never even considered doing something like that before. It marked so many *firsts* for me, you know? First time leaving Michigan, first time on a plane, first time on such a long camping and hiking trip… and my first time with you." Naomi beamed, her smile growing big and joyful.

"I can really feel the change in you," Gretchen said. "You're so much more confident now. So much stronger. You *are* Nova. And you're *not* burning out, you're still flaming bright and blazing through the sky. You're an absolute celestial *wonder.*" Naomi laughed and shook her head.

"Thanks," she said. "I'll take it."

"It's true," Gretchen confirmed with an earnest smile. "I'm happy to be with you on your journey." Reaching out, she indicated that she wanted Naomi's hand, and Naomi gladly gave it to her. Gretchen squeezed affectionately and she gazed at Naomi in adoration for a few expectant moments.

"We should go for a hike after this," Naomi said. "Just in the preserve around the complex."

"Yeah, totally," Gretchen agreed. "I would definitely be down with that."

"Are you going to miss having so much free time during the week to yourself?" asked Naomi.

"I will," said Gretchen. "But you know, there's so much more to life than just trying to live easy and put recreation above all else. Despite how free I've felt in living like that, I also have felt like I've fallen behind a bit. I don't know. I'd say it's a delicate balance, a balance I'm still searching for. It might be nice to have a little structure in my life again."

"You know, for me," Naomi added. "I feel like I'm finally becoming an adult. I know that's stupid and silly and that I've been an adult for a long time. A decade, really. I just… *wasn't*, you know? I wasn't living my life, I wasn't moving forward. I was stuck. But I feel so unstuck now and I feel like things are really happening for me. Who knows where this could all go. But it just feels right. It feels like I'm… *doing it.*"

"Instead of it doing you," Gretchen posited.

"Exactly," said Naomi. "That's exactly it."

"I'm so happy for you," said Gretchen. "And happy for me, too. We're figuring this out together and it's so exciting and rewarding. I don't know where I'd be headed if it weren't for you, Naomi. It makes me smile until it hurts when I think about how this all ended up, and how it might not have worked out like this. Maybe you didn't come with me to Maine, or maybe you didn't feel confident coming out. Where would we be then?"

"Probably still working at Dune City, dreaming about each other," Naomi said. "And just living life as friends instead of lovers."

"Yeah, that's probably right," Gretchen confirmed. "That's probably exactly what it would be."

"I'm not afraid anymore," Naomi said proudly. "If I can hike a hundred miles in the wilderness, with nothing but a backpack and my best friend by my side, there's nothing I can't do. I'm ready for whatever challenges come next. I'm ready to live my life."

"Me too," said Gretchen. She smiled, and she realized that she and Naomi were still holding hands. Leaning over and off of her chair, Gretchen closed in on Naomi and the girls kissed. It felt nice in the early autumn sun. So nice that they kissed a few more times before sitting back in their chairs and readjusting themselves.

"I'm going to take a dip," Naomi said, widening her legs and placing her feet on the concrete below. "You want to come with me?"

"Yep," said Gretchen.

Together the girls stood up from their chairs and prepared for the pool, removing their sunglasses, adjusting their bathing suits. Naomi came around from the other side of the chair and she leaned in and hugged Gretchen. They stood their hugging for a moment before walking together, hand in hand, over to the pool.

"Swim," said Gretchen. "And then a hike."

"And then a hike," Naomi agreed with a laugh.

They kissed once more at poolside, and then together they jumped in, disrupting the still water and forcing a splash. Coolness covered their warm bodies as they submerged. Under the water, Gretchen opened her eyes and saw Naomi there next to her. Naomi, her eyes open as well, was grinning wide. As she began swimming, pulling herself up toward the surface, Gretchen diligently swam after her. And as they breached, they held to one another, laughing and smiling. It was such a bright day, only made brighter by the rays of happiness that shimmered off of these two lovers.

When Naomi entered their bedroom, she was naked and still dewy from her shower with a white towel wrapped around her head. Gretchen was in bed, wearing just a pink pair of panties, and looking down into her phone. With Naomi's arrival, however, the phone was tossed aside. It had been such a wonderful and relaxing day. An afternoon at the pool, a hike around the local nature preserve, and a satisfying homemade dinner of whitefish and wine all culminated in subsequent showers and now this. The fading dusk sunlight shown in through their open bedroom window, along with a cool evening breeze.

Pulling the towel off and tossing it to the ground, Naomi shook her head side to side to let her hair down. Over the summer, Naomi's pale body had darkened as much as it could, leaving tan lines along her chest and her middle. She crept closer to the bed as Gretchen shot insinuating glances her way.

"Put on some music," Naomi intoned gently. "You know I like music."

"Mm hmm," Gretchen agreed. As Naomi climbed up onto the bed, Gretchen took up her phone once more, swiped through it, and then tapped a few times. A small wireless speaker on her nightstand came to life with low, dreamy, electronic pop music. The beat was steady and firm.

"Why are you still wearing these?" Naomi asked, tugging at the elastic of Gretchen's underwear.

"I really don't know," Gretchen said with a laugh. "Take them off."

"Gladly," Naomi said. She grabbed at the panties and she deftly pulled them down Gretchen's legs and took them off of her feet. She then tossed them blindly over her shoulder and moved closer once more to Gretchen. Leaning in, she planted a sweet kiss on Gretchen and Gretchen eagerly returned the affection.

Gretchen wriggled back into the bed to get comfortable and she spread her legs wider. The girls kissed some more, while Naomi's hand moved down and explored between her lover's thighs. With a happy groan, Gretchen melted into Naomi's touch and found her arousal mounting quickly. As Naomi's fingers kneaded and massaged, Gretchen easily grew wet with excitement.

"I love your body," Naomi mused. She lowered herself

slightly and pushed her mouth to Gretchen's tit, taking in her nipple and sucking it, ending with a tender bite. This sent an energetic shock through Gretchen and she couldn't help but giggle. Goosebumps appeared on her arms.

"You can do whatever you want to it," Gretchen hummed. She was dissolving into the lust, her limbs relaxing, her love tingling and growing wetter still.

"Don't mind if I do," Naomi teased. After kissing Gretchen's navel softly, she shimmied down between Gretchen's legs and enthusiastically started up. Naomi buried her face into Gretchen's pussy, pushing her lips sloppily into Gretchen's, kissing and licking and sucking flesh. Releasing her tongue, she flicked against Gretchen's clit before giving it a full, deep, vocal kiss. Naomi had gotten good at eating pussy and she was happy to demonstrate.

"Damn," Gretchen mewed, reaching her hand down and running it through Naomi's damp hair. She could feel the dampness of that hair on her thighs, but it was nowhere near as wet as what was going on between them.

"You like it?" Naomi asked between kisses.

"I love it."

"Good," Naomi said, and then gave another pressured kiss to Gretchen's clit.

Gretchen eventually flipped over, perched on her knees, and buried her head into the pillows. Her ass hung in the air, and Naomi was behind it, spreading her cheeks and licking everywhere. For a moment, Naomi pulled back and admired her lover's pussy glistening in the low light of the room. She smiled to herself and reached out to touch it, a bead of gooey sweetness dripped from Gretchen's lips and slowly made its way down to the sheets.

"You're so wet," Naomi said. "You're dripping."

"Don't stop," Gretchen pleaded with impatience. Naomi laughed.

"Sorry," she replied in a teasing voice. She again dove in, parting Gretchen's lips with her tongue and licking furiously. Moving upwards, she licked herself to Gretchen's ass which Gretchen, if her noises and movements were any indication, obviously loved.

With her hand between Gretchen's legs, fingers fondling her clit, Naomi's mouth moved back and forth along Gretchen's crevice. Gretchen's hips were gyrating and her breath was growing more fierce, she was gasping for air as her arousal became impossible to ignore. Soon, she was bucking and Naomi slapped one hand on her ass cheek and squeezed, all while maintaining a steady and firm licking of her pussy.

"Oh God," Gretchen called into a pillow. "Mmm!" She was exploding, and it was all the more magical and powerful as Naomi just wouldn't let up.

Gretchen was shaking, and Naomi finally pulled back to admire her work. She grinned to herself, still feeling an intense lust as Gretchen's backside stared back at her. Bringing her hand up, she used the back of it to wipe her mouth, and then wiped that hand on her own thigh. Naomi then smacked Gretchen's ass a few times coaxing a few more groans out of her beautiful best friend.

"I think I'm getting the hang of this," Naomi quipped. Gretchen replied with an exhausted laugh.

"Yeah, I'd say so," she said after a moment. "Holy shit, babe. I'm still tingling from that."

Gretchen then rolled over on her back and smiled up at Naomi, who was still looking down and admiring her lithe and supple body. The girls' eyes met and they stared at one another for a tender moment, both wearing joyous smiles on their faces.

"You're so sexy," Naomi said. "It's hard not to go full steam. I just want to rip you apart in bed," she said, wrapping her arms around herself, overcome with desire. "Mm mmm!"

"The beast is out," Gretchen joked. "Lots of pent up lust in that body of yours."

"You don't know the *half* of it," replied Naomi, laughing at herself. "Masturbating to thoughts of you is nowhere *near* the real thing."

"You masturbated to me?" Gretchen said with wide-eyed excitement. "For real?"

"Oh yeah," said Naomi. "A lot. But now I don't have to." She smiled sweetly.

"That's awesome," mused Gretchen. "Wow. I love it. Great for my ego, you know." Naomi laughed.

"Yep," she said. Leaning in, she kissed Gretchen a few times gently before shifting herself downward and pressing their bodies together. They lay there idly, kissing each other slowly and with fondness.

After some lazy moments of touching and kissing, their bodies feeling tacky with sweat as they lay together, Gretchen felt a new wave of energy and she jumped up from bed and ambled into the closet. Naomi flipped around, she now laying on her back, with her head tilted to watch Gretchen. She knew full well what was on Gretchen's mind when she went into the closet and Naomi waited with excited interest all over her face.

"Here it is," said Gretchen from the closet. Stepping back into the bedroom, she held a large white massage wand in her hand, with a thick base and a round bulbous head on it. Naomi grew physically excited and she squirmed in anticipation.

"The magic wand," said Naomi happily. "Gimme gimme!" Gretchen laughed as she climbed onto the bed, holding the wand aloft.

"Keep your pants on," teased Gretchen.

"I'm not wearing pants," Naomi shot back, giving Gretchen another laugh.

"Oh," she said, feigning surprise. "I guess you're not."

Gretchen swung a leg over Naomi and mounted her, sitting upright on Naomi's thighs. Naomi watched with thrill, squirming a bit in anticipation. She had her arms crossed over her chest, her own nipples between her fingers, giving them expectant squeezes. Gretchen then turned the magic wand around so that the bulbous head was pointed downward and she lowered it further and began positioning it between them.

Resting the head of the massager on Naomi's clit,

Gretchen adjusted herself so that her pussy pressed against the other side of it.

"Turn it on," Naomi beckoned. "Come on. Turn it on."

"You ready?" Gretchen asked slowly, with a teasing grin.

"Yes!"

"Okay," replied Gretchen simply. Reaching down to the wand's base, she flipped a switch and the head began vibrating firmly. They both began to shiver with the vibrations.

"Oh my God," Naomi called out, bending at her middle and sitting up for a beat. She then dropped back and dissolved into the pleasure. Gretchen grinned wide and held the wand steady, she too melting with the reverberations. The heat between them grew as quickly as their wet arousal.

This was the life of freedom they both had desired, and this love between two best friends was more than either could have hoped for. Naomi felt as though she could be wide open with Gretchen, and that meant the world to her. And Gretchen, finding a partner in Naomi, discovered balance in the lifestyle she was trying to achieve. Their love was powerful and bright, and it burst out between them in what felt like a vibrant rainbow of cascading colors. They squirmed and quivered together, as one, happily reveling in their devotion to one another, an escalating bliss, and a fulfilling and sweaty climax.

Together, these women were unstoppable. And they knew it.

EPILOGUE

A few months later, in December…

IT WAS cold in the desert, but the girls were smiling big as they watched the sunrise over a large sandstone arch, each of them cradling a steaming cup of coffee. It was Nova's thirtieth birthday and they had made the trek out to Moab, Utah and Arches National Park. When Nova had suggested the trip, Piggy laughed at her and asked if she knew that the desert got winter, too. Nova just shrugged and smiled and said she wanted to do it anyway. So that's what they did.

They were both bundled up in puffy jackets, wool hats, and wearing climbing pants but neither wore socks underneath their sandals. The high desert of Arches with its deep red sand indeed succumbed to winter, though fortunately it hadn't snowed on the girls' trip. Still, overnight, sleeping in their tent, they covered up in thick down sleeping bags and cuddled together to stay warm. After stargazing up into the immensely dark sky populated with more stars than either had seen in their lives, of course.

Nova wanted to try bouldering for her birthday—free-climbing small rock formations without the use of any kind of harness or rope—and that was their plan for the day. The proceeding days were spent hiking through the various trails in the park, and reveling in the sight of all those amazing sandstone arches. There were over two thousand arches in the park, and it never got old seeing another one. They were ecological marvels, always awe-inspiring.

But on the morning of her birthday, Nova cuddled up against Piggy, the two of them seated next to one another on a rock, trying to keep warm, drink their coffee, and enjoy the sunrise. It felt magical. It felt like they were exactly where they were supposed to be.

"I told you the desert would be cold," Piggy teased, grinning as she leaned over and kissed Nova on the cheek.

"At least we'll get to try out climbing a few boulders we wouldn't get to do in the summer, Nova replied. "I read that it gets way to hot in the summer for some of them."

"Right," said Piggy. "I'm excited for that. This is my first time bouldering, too."

"And God, the hiking out here is incredible," said Nova. "Pictures do not do this place justice. I feel like I'm inexplicably drawn to the beauty out here in the desert. We should just move here." Piggy laughed.

"Maybe one day," she said. "Though we do have a lot going for us back in Traverse City."

"I'm just excited," Nova said with a big grin. "I love this. I love that we got to come out here for my birthday, and I love you."

"I love you, too," said Piggy. They kissed slowly and tenderly, ending their kiss with comfortable and confident smiles.

"Do you think we'll see any desert snow?" Nova asked.

"I don't know," said Piggy. "At first, I felt like… no way do I want it to snow on us. But being out here, seeing what the landscape is like, now I think it would be really pretty if we saw some snow."

"Right?" agreed Nova. "I think it would be supremely pretty. I'm kind of hoping it snows."

"We have a few more days out here," said Piggy. "It could happen."

"I love being out here and camping," Nova continued, smiling as she looked out onto the horizon. "It's like being in a different world. It's so simple and so freeing."

"And we found a spot to camp with nobody else around," added Piggy, looking around them to remind herself of how remote they were.

"You're all I need," Nova said, leaning her head down and resting it on Piggy's shoulder.

"Aw," said Piggy. She kissed Nova's wool hat.

"I'm so happy about so much lately," Nova went on. "This new job has been great, my parents are finally coming around and treating me normal again, I love having my own apartment—I mean, living with *you*, of course—it just seems like everything is going my way, and I'm so grateful that I get to live all this. For the first time in my life, I feel really, truly, authentically *happy*. I was hiding from so much of myself, and now that I'm not anymore… everything has gotten better."

"You are an amazing person, Naomi," Piggy said. "And I'm so happy that you're really getting your chance to shine bright."

Nova smiled as she looked into Piggy's eyes. Piggy and Nova, Gretchen and Naomi, they were all one in the same. But sometimes it takes getting out of your element, out of your comfort zone, and donning an alternative moniker to find out who you really are. For Naomi, taking that chance on a trip to the wilderness, allowing herself to be someone else—if only for a week—had been the key to realizing that she wasn't being someone else at all. Away from everything she knew, she finally got a chance to be herself. And once she saw who she truly was, there was no going back.

The girls had discovered a great love of exploring the unknown together, and no longer was Naomi afraid of what the unknown might hold. Heading out on a trail, whether in the woods or in the desert or anything in-between, was always an adventure worth having. There was always something new to see, always something different to survey. And Gretchen, too, was excited for what the trail might reveal. She had found balance with Naomi, and Gretchen knew it would be that balance in her lifestyle that would help her move forward and find her way.

"I really like being able to shine," mused Naomi tenderly. "I think everybody needs to find their shine. It's so important to discovering your true happiness. If you're always hiding, you'll never get there."

"You're not hiding anymore," said Gretchen, feeling the happiness emanate from Naomi. "And I can see it all over your face how happy you are."

"I am happy," Naomi agreed. "So, so happy."

Naomi smiled, and they looked at one another for a few joyful moments. Then, Naomi leaned in and pressed her lips firmly to Gretchen's, the two of them kissing once again as the sun continued to climb the horizon. The desert was cold, but there was intense warmth between Gretchen and Naomi. And it was a fire that would surely burn bright, like a celestial blaze in the sky, for as long as there was a sky above.

Thank You!

A Note From Nicolette Dane

I JUST WANT to thank you so much for your readership. I write these novels for you, and I sincerely do hope you enjoy them. If you did enjoy this story, I would really appreciate it if you left a review of the book. Reviews are very important to the success of a book, and your review could help me reach more readers. Even if you're not the wordy type, leaving a review saying "I really enjoyed this book!" is still incredibly helpful.

I have so much more for you to read. Keep going through this book to see some of my personal recommendations. If you enjoyed this story, I am positive you'll love my other stories as well.

Again, thank you from the bottom of my heart.

Love,

Nico

If you want to be notified
of all new releases from Nico,
sign up for her mailing list today
and get 3 FREE BOOKS!

Point your web browser
to the following address
and sign up right now!

www.nicolettedane.com

Keep reading to see more books from
Nicolette Dane!

EXIT STRATEGY

Mae Huxley runs a budding tech start-up in Detroit, with the mission of getting more girls into computer programming. But she's hit a snag. In the midst of a new project that promises to spread her teachings worldwide, Mae and her business are running out of money.

Through a bit of serendipity, Mae is connected with one of her idols—wealthy technology goddess Audrey Addison. Audrey worked for the biggest tech giant out there, and now she owns her own angel investment firm. But she's a serious and severe woman, a keen business mind, and she's known to be an ice queen despite her fiery red hair.

As they grow the company together, Mae sees through Audrey's stern reputation and discovers the real woman underneath. Can Mae melt Audrey's heart and succeed both in business and in love?

Follow The Link To See More
www.nicolettedane.com

FLOWER POWER

Taryn Donaghy's job as an equities trader at a financial services firm is leading her down a dark road. The long hours and the high pressure are taking a toll on her mental health. Taryn knows she needs a change, but she doesn't know what that change looks like or how to find it.

A chance meeting with Alex Maris, a florist who delivers a flower feature to the office every week, opens Taryn's eyes and shows her a different path. Alex lives and works on a co-op farm with others like her, a sort of hippie collective of people doing their own thing. It's hard for Taryn not to be intrigued by Alex. She's beautiful and kind, and she's living the blissful and fulfilled life that Taryn is after.

If Taryn doesn't figure her path out soon she might just break down. Will Alex and her farm show Taryn how to find herself and find the love that's eluded her for so long?

Follow The Link To See More

www.nicolettedane.com

LADY PILOT

Captain Elaine Cole is an accomplished and popular commercial airline pilot. She's spent her entire career bouncing from one airport to the next, and one lover to the next as well. Being a pilot has made it hard for Lanie to settle down and find love, and now that she's in her forties it's really starting to wear on her.

When Carrie Haden is assigned as a flight attendant on her route, Lanie feels herself falling for the beautiful younger woman. But Carrie is different than the flight attendants Lanie has been with in the past. There's something else there—a brighter spark, a deeper affection—and Lanie can't help but feel that this is her opportunity to finally find the love she seeks.

Building trust and committing to a relationship is difficult for a pilot like Lanie. Could Carrie be the one who finally inspires Lanie to change her ways?

Follow The Link To See More

www.nicolettedane.com

HIDDEN TREASURES

Looking to leave her troubled past behind her, Annie Arbuckle takes a restaurant job in the northern resort town of Traverse City, far away from everything and everyone she knows. Annie needs change, a break from the party girl life she had in Detroit, and spending summer in this small town of vacationers seems like the perfect way to get her life back on track.

Then she meets Nora Lowe. Nora is a server at the restaurant, she's gorgeous, curvy, exciting, with a bit of a wild streak. Things don't always add up with Nora, she often seems to be hiding something, but Annie has a hard time saying no to someone so beautiful and so fun. And that can get her into trouble.

Now, with new love on the line, will Annie be able to avoid falling back into old habits while maintaining her budding relationship with Nora? Or will the mischief and the secrets that Nora clings to push Annie over the edge?

Follow The Link To See More
www.nicolettedane.com

CHIEF EXECUTIVE

Nadia Marek, a graphic designer and account manager at a boutique advertising agency, is about to have her work life flipped upside down. A major competitor has bought her company out and with this shakeup comes the arrival of a new CEO. Nadia's fears for the future of her job become more complicated, however, when she discovers how attracted she is to her new boss.

That boss is Avery Wool, a confident and strong executive, who has come in to reorganize the company. But Avery appears to have ulterior motives. As the changes begin to take hold, things aren't always what they seem with Avery. Nadia, however, can't help but fall for Avery's advances.

She's a beautiful woman, sultry, powerful, rich… and she has Nadia in her sights.

How will Nadia reconcile her feelings about the corporate takeover with the growing desire she feels for her new CEO? Is the mounting passion between the women for real, or is it all just a game to Avery? Work often takes a backseat when you have romance knocking at your office door.

Follow The Link To See More

www.nicolettedane.com

FIELD DAY

After getting into some trouble in the big city, Jane Cairns is sent to live with her aunt and uncle on the family farm in southwest Michigan. Jane's living in a state of arrested development, ambling through young adulthood and finding it difficult to flourish on her own. She just can't get her act together.

When she meets Sally Harris, a local farmer who works on her family's cherry orchard, Jane sees in her new friend a responsible young woman who has it figured out. But Sally, too, has her struggles. Where she's from, it's hard for her to be herself and be open about her desires.

As they each battle their own issues of identity and

place, love begins to flourish for Jane and Sally. But can their budding affection survive a dirty past, a secret relationship, family conflict, and more?

Follow The Link To See More
www.nicolettedane.com

A WAY WITH WORDS

Evelyn Driscoll, famed novelist and professor at a small midwestern arts college, is in a rut. It's been over seven years since her hit book came out, her editor is clamoring for a new manuscript, and life in northern Ohio just doesn't compare to the literary world she once inhabited. Her love life feels like even more of a mess.

When one of Evie's graduate students—the beautiful and talented Meadow Sims—admits that she's got a thing for her professor, Evie feels her lost passion start to come back. Meadow is smart, sweet, and has almost finished a novel of her own. The two must write their story carefully, however, as dating a student could put Evie's teaching career at risk.

With Meadow by her side, Evie's inspiration is blooming once again. But can this May-December romance succeed despite the professional consequences?

Follow The Link To See More

www.nicolettedane.com

AN ACT OF LOVE

When Jessica Coleridge arrives in Los Angeles to open her new yoga studio, the only person she knows in town is her old friend Liberty Logan. To Jessica's surprise, Liberty has become a famous actress on a hit television show. As the friends rekindle what they once had, romance begins to blossom and this reunion quickly evolves into something much more than friendship.

But fame and money begin to play tricks on Liberty, as she's still naive to her growing celebrity. And with Jessica reentering her life out of the blue, Liberty has a difficult time determining what's real and what's just an act. When money and business mix with love and romance, even old friends can find trust to be a difficult proposition.

With love on the line, both women need to figure out who they are and what they want. Can this second chance at love for Jessica and Liberty win out over the trappings of Hollywood, fame, and money?

Follow The Link To See More
www.nicolettedane.com

AN EXCERPT: LADY PILOT

Chicago O'Hare International Airport, or ORD for short, was bustling with passengers waiting to board their flights. The airport was a grand construction, with steel girders lining the ceiling and separated by glass windows, morning light shining down into the immense building. As far as airports go, it was quite beautiful. But most people didn't seem to notice. Most people rushed about, trying to quickly move from security to their terminal so that they could plop down in a seat and wait to board, as though that would get them to their destination faster.

Hanging around Gate B10 in Terminal 1 was a flight crew. They were smiling, chatting, occasionally laughing as though they knew each other well. There were five of them together. One, a man in his late thirties, was dressed in a pilot's uniform and was leading the group. He was animated and excited, bright-eyed and plucky. This was Stephen Reynolds, the co-pilot.

"I told my boyfriend," he said with a quick hand gesture. "Play your cards right, dear, and *maybe* I won't replace you with a young cabana boy."

The group laughed along with him. There was Beth, a woman about the same age as Stephen. She had her dark hair pulled back in a tight ponytail, her large chest squeezed into her flight attendant uniform. Next to her was Hugh, a chubby man with dark glasses, spiky hair, and a goatee. And Tanya, African-American, her black hair straightened and pulled back just as tightly as Beth's. This group, along with Stephen, was obviously close. But standing with them, almost like an outcast with a smile on her face as though she was just playing along, was a woman in her early thirties with light brown hair worn down. Her uniform conveyed her fitness underneath, along with her curves, but her expression revealed her trepidation.

"C'mon Carrie," said Stephen, offering this young woman another flourishing gesture with his hand. "I'm *hilarious*."

"You are," replied Carrie, giving Stephen a smile. Stephen rolled his eyes dramatically.

"Where's Captain Cole?" Tanya asked, shifting the subject. "They look like they're about ready to open the gate for us."

"*Psssh*," said Stephen. "Probably nursing a hangover."

The group—everyone but Carrie—laughed.

"Oh, stop it," said Beth. "We're lucky to have Captain Cole. And this route, a Chicago to Cancun turnaround, is like a dream. Passengers will be happy and excited on the way there, exhausted and tired on the way back. Captain Cole made this happen for us."

"Captain Cole *this*, Captain Cole *that*," mused Stephen, twirling a finger in the air.

"Captain Cole is great," said Hugh. "I'm a fan."

"Oh!" said Tanya. "There she is now."

As the crew all looked down the terminal, they saw the captain heading their way. Captain Elaine Cole, or just Lanie to her friends, strutted toward them pulling a wheeled suitcase behind her with a bemused smile on her lips. Her blonde hair bounced against her shoulders with each step, a captain's hat fitted atop her head. She was shapely yet trim, her uniform unable to obscure her blessings. Lanie was beautiful, sexy and seductive, and she knew it. Even in her early 40s, she exuded a youthfulness that could often get her in trouble.

Lanie approached the crew and released her suitcase. She grinned.

"I told the airline I wanted *professionals*," Lanie teased. "But I guess you all will do."

They laughed at her quip.

"Captain Cole," said Hugh. "We're all really looking forward to this assignment. We're so lucky to get on this route."

"I've been working on it for ages," said Lanie. "Pleading my case, kissing up to the boss, putting in my time. And here we are," she said, smiling big as she considered her accomplishment. "Three turnarounds to Cancun a week. The days will be long, but having four days off is going to be so sweet. And I'll finally get to start *living* for once." She laughed.

"I don't know how you did it," said Beth. "And we're so grateful you've brought us along for the ride."

"Captain Cole is the greatest, isn't she?" said Stephen, cuddling up to Lanie and hugging her.

"You said she was going to come in here hungover," protested Hugh. Stephen's eyes widened and he put his finger to his lips to shush Hugh. But Lanie laughed.

"Bottle to throttle is twelve hours," said Lanie. "Those are the rules I live by. On my days off, well, that's a different story."

Lanie maintained an easy smile as she looked over her crew. But when her eyes reached Carrie, she furrowed her brow. Carrie was young and pretty, quite fresh looking, but she also appeared uneasy and uncertain about the group she found herself in.

"You must be Carolyn Haden," said Lanie. She reached her hand out to shake. "Nice to meet you."

"It's nice to meet you, Captain," said Carrie. She shook.

"It turned out that Peggy's husband got transferred to San Diego for work," said Lanie. "So Peggy is no longer calling ORD homebase. And we've been assigned Miss Haden, here. Miss Haden, you are very lucky to be among one of the best flight crews to ever fly on AmeriNorth

Airlines. I know they look like misfits, but they clean up nice." The group laughed, and Carrie smiled demurely at her captain.

"I'm looking forward to this assignment," said Carrie.

Lanie looked over Carrie once again, and her lips maintained a curled smile. Carrie was charming and alluring in her caution. Despite the attraction that Lanie felt for her new flight attendant, she had promised herself that she wouldn't make that mistake again. No more flight attendants for her.

"I, too, am looking forward to this assignment," replied Lanie, but addressing the entire crew. "I'm hoping to move past the days of waking up in a different city every morning, unsure where I am exactly. And I feel like I'm getting a bit too old for our little party scene. I'm ready to turn in my keys to all the crash pads and delete a few phone numbers from my phone. We're going to do this, team. It's going to be great."

"I'm just looking forward to a narrowbody full of happy people," said Tanya. "Look at them all," she said, motioning toward the passengers sitting near the gate. Despite the early hour, people looked happy and were in good spirits, many already dressed in beach clothes. It was early spring, the snow was just beginning to melt, and not a winter coat could be seen. There would be no use for a coat in Cancun. "Going off to a beach vacation is the best thing ever. Happy passengers make our job so much easier."

"Don't get ahead of yourself, Tanya," warned Lanie. "We're bound to get some rowdy people who can't wait to get hammered until they hit the beach. But I do think we're in for some fun times."

A woman in a navy blazer and skirt walked up to the crew and smiled. She was an ANA gate agent and she waited patiently until the crew stopped their conversation and looked her way.

"Captain Cole," said the woman. "We're ready for you."

"Thank you, Sarah," said Lanie. "All right, gang. Let's do this."

The flight crew cheered. They took up their rolling suitcases and, lead by Stephen, began walking toward the now-open gate door. The gate agent standing at the podium greeted each one as they walked through.

The last two to prepare themselves to board were Lanie and Carrie. Lanie wanted to wait for her entire crew to board before she did, and Carrie felt that she should take up the rear as the newest member of the team. Lanie looked to her and smiled gently.

"I know they can be a bit much," said Lanie. "But they're a good team. Really good at their jobs. Fun and accepting. I don't think many people—pilots or flight attendants alike—get an opportunity to fly with such a great crew on such a great route. You got a good gig here."

"I know," Carrie said. She smiled. "I'm trying not to take it for granted. I've only been a flight attendant for a few years. I lucked out to get an assignment like this."

"You should send Peggy a very nice gift," Lanie teased. Carrie laughed.

"Maybe I will," said Carrie.

Both women stood there for a moment, waiting for the other one to take the lead. After a pause, Lanie widened her eyes and motioned toward the boarding gate with her hand.

"Oh no," said Carrie. "After you, Captain Cole."

"You first, I insist," said Lanie, smiling contently. "And you can call me Lanie."

"Call you Lanie?"

"Well, yeah," said Lanie. "I mean, when it's just us. In front of passengers and the crew, Captain Cole is good. But when it's you and I, Lanie is what I prefer."

"Okay," replied Carrie. "You can call me Carrie."

"After you, Carrie," said Lanie, still smiling. She motioned once again with her hand. Carrie laughed softly, she took the handle of her rolling suitcase, and she made her way to the open gate. Lanie paused for a moment and watched her walk off. Dirty thoughts percolated in her head, and Lanie immediately chastised herself.

"New you," Lanie said under her breath as she now began her walk through the door. "Be good, Lanie. Be good."

Follow The Link To See More

www.nicolettedane.com

Made in the USA
Coppell, TX
15 October 2020